FORGOTTEN

By Samie Sands

Samie Sands

FORGOTTEN

First Print Edition: May 2016

Limitless Publishing, LLC
Kailua, HI 96734
www.limitlesspublishing.com

Formatting: Limitless Publishing

ISBN-13: 978-1-68058-605-3
ISBN-10: 1-68058-605-X

DEDICATION

For James and Akira.

PROLOGUE

Bang.

That noise.

Bang. Bang.

So loud. It feels like it's coming from inside my own head.

Bang.

I cover my ears with my hands, pulling my knees up to my chest, trying to block out the whole world for a moment. I just need to *think*.

I don't know what to do about her, I really don't. I can't just do *nothing*. She isn't right, however much I try to convince myself otherwise. I have to accept the truth. I have to admit that whatever is behind that door isn't my cousin. Not anymore. But that doesn't make this any easier.

When I found her, outside the door collapsed and covered in blood, I completely freaked out, what if she had this *thing*, the illness? I had to block out all my deep-rooted fears about catching the disease while I carried her in and cleaned her off. I didn't have any choice, did I? There's no one else left—as far as I'm aware, anyway. I don't even know *how* she got here. Was she heading this way on purpose, coming to see me? Or was it simply a coincidence that it's my door she passed out in front of?

I left her to sleep. She slept for days. She slept for so long I started to fear that I was too late, that she was already dead.

Then, there was movement.

I heard her get up out of the bed and move about the room. I waited. I didn't talk for fear of what she might say, for fear of learning what had truly happened to her.

She switched. Day to day. Minute to minute. One moment she would be speaking, albeit very slurred and stilted words that I could never really understand. The next I'd just hear screaming and smashing, as things would be thrown around in a violent rage. It was terrifying.

Now, I'd give anything for that emotion. Now all I can hear is growling, moaning, shuffling.

And banging.

Bang. Bang. Bang.

I fear she's going to bring that flimsy door down soon, making my decision for me. I'm not ready for that, not yet. I've already lost too many people. She might be the only one I have left.

I already know that my parents are dead. The last time I spoke to my mother, I could hear my dad slowly dying in the background. He was coughing and spluttering the whole time, and growling in between. He was starting to sound just like all the others do—the infected on the outside. I could hear the trepidation in Mum's voice, but she wouldn't tell me any details. I'm sure she must have known that neither of them had much time left, but she was too proud to let me help.

I could have done it anyway, I suppose. When I tried to call over the next few days and got no answer, I could have hot footed over there and helped them both out, but I didn't. I'm a coward—I always have been—but that doesn't stop the guilt from eating me up. I was too afraid of finding them both hungry for my flesh. I was terrified of joining them in the undead army that's growing steadily by the minute.

I think it's safe to say that the Lockdown has failed.

The Lockdown. What an idea—quarantine everyone inside their own homes, gather all the infected into a specialised medical facility to cure them, and then let life get back to normal.

That's what we were led to believe was the plan. Unfortunately, it hasn't seemed to work out that way at all. I don't know what went wrong—how or why—but here we are. The number of infected roaming the streets is rising rapidly, and no one has any idea what's going to happen next. There's never any new information on the television or radio; the news reports are just repeats from before. There are definitely no signs of life returning to normality any time soon.

If I was still receiving food deliveries from the armed forces, I might feel a little bit better about the whole thing, but they petered out a while ago, just proving to me that this has gotten out of control. I'm rapidly losing confidence in any of us surviving this mess. I think the AM13 virus was ravaging far too out of control before the government even attempted to get a handle on it. I don't think they ever stood a chance against it; they'd left it far too late.

Oh Leah, I wish you weren't behind that door, banging away. I wish you were on this side, with me, helping me get through this. I've only just managed to scrub all of your blood from my skin. You can just imagine how bad that was for me, can't you? But I did it for you, because you're my family and I love you. I keep reminiscing, remembering us playing together as children, and looking after each other throughout school. I can't get my head around the fact that my lovely cousin Leah is that violent beast in the other room. It's too sad to comprehend.

CHAPTER 1

Race

ETHAN

"This is crazy, it's absolutely insane." I've gotten to the point of talking to myself, which I know is a terrible sign. I've been wandering around for a few days now, too terrified to stop for even a second, never mind sleep. I think my mind is starting to lose it a bit with hunger and exhaustion. I'm starting to regret my snap decision to leave the house; but I just couldn't bear to sit there waiting for death any longer. I've never made a quick choice before, I always deliberate things for a very long time, analysing it all from every possible angle. Certain people used to criticise me for it, but the first time I break out of that mould, *this* happens.

I can't go back home though, no way. I wouldn't be able to bear it. Not only is my house a constant reminder of everything I've lost, every breath I take inside those four walls is dangerous. The virus is all over the walls in that building, it's clinging to the air. I could feel it starting to seep through my skin, trying to work its way into me. I was feeling ill, convincing myself that I had AM13, even though I wasn't displaying any signs at all. I can't control the hypochondriac that lingers in my brain, constantly nagging at me, never leaving me alone.

I really want to find another house to stay in. This is just as bad, if not worse, as the situation I was in before. Out here I'm always vulnerable. There's constantly something after me, even if I can't see it. The smell lingering in the air is rotten and disgusting, which makes me feel sick to my stomach, and I've already used up all of my hand sanitizer that comes everywhere with me—I'm really on edge without it. I keep subconsciously walking with my hands held away from me, as if I want to separate them from my body. If I could find somewhere new to stay, I could eat, drink, and wash. Plus, it would also be incredibly useful to gain access to the news. I know nothing new has been reported for a while now, but I don't want to miss it when it does.

Most of the houses look abandoned—I can't tell if this is a good thing…or a really bad one. I don't know if their owners picked somewhere else to hole up during the Lockdown, if they were forced out by starvation, or if they were early victims of the disease, and it's this lack of knowledge that's making me unsure of my next move. I need to work up the courage soon though, or I'll end up dying for sure. I *need* to be brave for just once in my life. I must do something positive. I haven't got anything to lose in any case—I've already lost everything.

I take in a deep breath, trying to ignore my pounding heart, trying to force myself to be decisive. I can't stay stuck inside my tiny bubble of fear any longer. I need to do the opposite of what I would usually do, and do something constructive. After all, this is literally a case of life or death. I shudder, taking faltering steps towards a building in an agonising decision-making process. I'm shaking, sweating; my feet feel like they aren't even touching the ground. I've never done anything like this before, ever, and the panic is curling tightly around my heart.

My fingers unfurl as I reach the innocuous door. There might be nothing out of the ordinary about this building, but it's the most important set of bricks that I'll ever be faced with in my entire life. It changes everything. If I can do *this*, if I can just get inside here and stay safe, I'll be able to do anything. I'll be able to slowly release myself from the grip of the Obsessive Compulsive Disorder that has restricted my entire existence up to this point. I might *just* be able to survive this disease that could possibly threaten humans into extinction.

Oh God, I need to stop thinking things like that. I've got to try to shut off my doomsday inner voice. It's making everything feel so much worse than it already is—and that's saying something in this nightmare!

I force my fingers forward, the butterflies in my stomach becoming more like large birds. The tension is too much; the sweat is already racing down my forehead. A noise, a slight shuffle makes me jump backwards, my heart in my throat. I push my ear up against the door, straining to hear over my own laboured breathing. Silence. I must have been imagining it. I can't let myself get worked up over nothing; it'll end up killing me. I gulp down some deep breaths of cool air before trying again.

The door swings open easily, too easily. It makes me think the previous occupants were forced to leave in a hurry. I hope that doesn't mean anything or—more importantly anyone—has been left behind. I shake my head, trying to clear out any negative thoughts, trying to focus. I've already taken a huge step today, a massive step. I don't want to backtrack over my own pessimistic mind.

I flick the light on, then off again, repeating the process three times, just to try to keep myself calm. I'm happy to still have electricity—I thought with the loss of control of the virus, we would also lose household commodities. I suppose that's one victory to be grateful for.

Well, for now at least…

"Hello?" I whisper quietly, too quietly for anyone to hear me. I clear my throat noisily and try again, willing my voice to come out louder. "Hello?" I can't keep the wobble from it, however much I try. It seems that the nerves aren't going anywhere anytime soon.

No one answers me but I still can't get myself to calm down. Not yet, not until I'm certain. I walk slowly on my tiptoes into each room, scanning each one thoroughly. Looking in every nook and cranny, just to check that no one is hiding. Each empty room brings with it crashing waves of relief. For someone like me, who struggles with even the simplest of everyday challenges, to be rewarded for my bravery is just mind blowing.

Soon, I am forced with one test too far. The attic. The dusty, mouldy attic that will be full to the brim with germs. Much as I tell myself that I've absolutely *no* reason to go up there, that it'll be empty, and even if it isn't, nothing threatening will have any way of getting to me, I can't stop thinking about it. Even as I'm in the kitchen scanning all the canned food that sits in the cupboards. Even as I'm eating a warm bowl of vegetable soup, wishing desperately that I had some bread to dip in it. Even as I'm washing up my dishes, I can't stop thinking about the attic.

I know I'll never get to sleep, however tired I am. I find it hard to switch off even at the best of times, so I'll never be able to stop this worry from buzzing in my ear. I *have* to do it. I need to make my way up that ladder and have a look. Just for a second. I won't need to be there for long. If I can just stop trembling, it'll be all over a lot quicker.

I stand at the bottom of the ladder tapping my foot. I can hear bangs and crashes coming from above me, but I know for a fact that they're nothing more than a construct of my mind. I *know* that, so why can't I just ignore them and go up there? Why am I frozen to the spot?

Each creaky step up the ladder is a milestone. I have to keep pausing to wait for my head to stop spinning, and for my heart rate to return to a bearable pace. I can do this, I *can*. After everything I've achieved today, this is nothing. This is simple, just a quick peek and then all will be fine. Nothing to worry about. All I need to do is take one deep breath, count to three and then force my head upwards.

* * *

As I see the steaming jets of water running from the shower, my spirits start to soar. I stare at my face in the mirror as it fogs over. Same jet black hair, same piercing blue eyes, same scar on my cheek that has been there since I fell climbing on rocks when I was ten. Nothing has physically changed, but I look like an entirely different person. Maybe it's just my perception that's new. Maybe it's because I'm slowly breaking out of my shell.

As I step under the flow and feel my muscles loosen, I smile to myself. I've done it, I've actually completed tasks that would have been impossible to me only days before. The attic was empty, completely unused, just like I knew it would be. There was dust, lots of it, but I'm washing that off now. I won't let my mind get tangled up and twisted in that, however much it wants to. I'm going to stay focused from now on. I've realised that when I push myself, nothing is impossible. Maybe this outbreak is *actually* going to be a good thing for me. It's possible that when this all blows over, I'll be able to live a more fulfilling life. My luck has been good to me today. This could be a sign of things to come.

CHAPTER 2

ALYSSA

My hands are trembling; my mouth dry, the knot in my stomach is so tight it threatens to encase my whole body. I've been sitting, frozen in a state of shock for God knows how long. I'm gripping onto the knife so hard its blade is cutting through the top layer of my skin, causing a thin trickle of blood to trail down my fingers.

What the fuck just happened?

My little sister lies dead at my feet, murdered by the kitchen knife in my hands. Killed by me. I can't even begin to get my head around what I've done, she is—*was* only eight years old. And such a petite, pretty thing. Blonde hair, bright turquoise eyes, chubby cheeks, a sweet smile, the whole works. I glance down at her frail, lifeless body. Bile rises up into my throat as my pulse races at an uncontrollable pace.

What a stupid bitch.

How could she have been so God damn

incredibly thick? I told her over and over again that if she went outside, she would die. That there was no other outcome. She'd sit there all meek, tears dripping from the corners of her eyes, listening to my instructions, nodding shyly, appearing to soak up my every word.

But no, she just had to go and do it, didn't she? She had to find out for herself. Well, she's learnt her lesson the hard way now. When I caught her, out in the garden, just standing there, I knew. I knew right then in that moment that we were over. That she was as dead as our parents. She turned around and dared to look me in the eyes, with an expression so defiant it actually took me back for a second. Then she stormed past me into the house, refusing to talk to me for days, however much I screamed and yelled. She knew I was frightened, she knew I was worried about losing her, and she just left me to stew. Even crying only resulted in silence, and I *never* cry. She's always known how to rile me up, that girl, but I've always loved her nonetheless. She's my sister, which only makes me more pissed off with the bad turn this took.

She eventually stumbled out of her room, pale, almost grey, and barely breathing. My blood ran cold as I automatically gripped onto the knife next to me, just waiting. Her eyes flicked up at me, the familiar colourless irises filled my heart with an overwhelming sadness, which I immediately forced myself to replace with a burning rage. How *dare* she let this happen to her? I spent all that effort trying to look after her, teaching her the best way to survive and for what? For her to take both our lives into her own hands? For her to allow her stupid decisions to affect my life as well as her own?

When this new version of my sister lunged for me, I sprang into action almost instantly. It didn't matter to me what or who she'd been, I've seen enough zombie films and read enough books to know that her past had gone, her personality was no more. That all she wanted to do now was to eat every scrap of flesh off my bones. Sentiment has no place in the apocalypse, everyone knows that.

I can still see the knife piercing her flesh. The blood…so much blood everywhere. I really had to force the blade to make it go into her brain deep enough to stop her. It isn't as easy as I'd assumed it would be. When an aggressive cannibal is close to scraping its teeth against your arm and you're pushing the weapon with all your might, just trying to break through the barrier, there's a second when you think you have no chance of making it. I was lucky really; I managed to keep my cool to get the job done. That's the first rule of survival, don't lose your head. Well, that and always be prepared.

Suddenly, a blood curdling scream shakes me out of my comatose state. That noise, it's burning my ears. I need to get it to stop. My chest is vibrating with the volume of it.

It's only when the knife clangs loudly to the floor that I realise the sound is coming from within me. All the pent up frustration and rage I've been feeling over the past few weeks have finally burst out of my chest. I aid these emotions by grabbing and throwing things, smashing whatever I can get my hands on. After forcing myself to be quiet for so long, it's nice to no longer care, to just yell and cause chaos. To not be cautious, to not be frightened.

When I eventually break off, panting, I let the past events fill my mind, just for a second, just to fuel my feelings further. Everyone ignored the warnings about AM13, everyone carried on as if life was normal, no one seemed to care that all their lives were at risk. Except me. I knew better. I've been expecting something like this for as long as I could remember, which is why I insisted on joining the Girl Guides when I was a child, to learn survivalist skills, and why I was so desperate to study martial arts.

Now the time for all that education to come in handy has arrived, just as I predicted.

As soon as I heard the first report on AM13, I started to spend my free time researching, trying to find out everything I could about it. I wanted as much knowledge as possible to go alongside my preparation. I wanted to be one of the few people who actually had the ability to survive what was starting to look more and more like the end of the world. I knew it was the right thing to do, and it seems now like I was one of the few smart ones.

I tried to impart my knowledge and wisdom on my friends and family, but was met with disdain and laughter. Everyone seemed convinced that it was just a media scare, even when the plans for the Lockdown were announced. Of course it was much more complicated than that, the government had never gone to these extremes over health issues before, why couldn't anyone else see that? Anyway, look who's laughing now. I can't imagine a single one of those people have survived this far. I bet I'm the only person left in this whole damn town. Well, fuck the lot of them, I'm not going to give anyone stupid enough to get themselves killed a second thought. No, now is the time to focus on me. It'll actually be nice to just be responsible for my own survival for a change.

CHAPTER 3

ETHAN

I'm pacing up and down the unfamiliar room, rubbing my hands together manically while I allow myself to get more and more stressed out. How the hell do they think they're going to pull this one off? I woke up from a restless sleep—I just couldn't relax properly in the strange environment—and flicked on the television. I didn't expect to see anything different, it's been rolling reports for such a long time, but this time I found myself presented with the brand new plan.

It seems they intend to fly all the remaining survivors from the UK to a 'secure destination' abroad. No details, no indication of where or how. Just the instructions to get ourselves to the nearest airport as soon as possible. Have they even thought this through at all, or is it just another knee jerk reaction like the Lockdown was? How do they expect us all to get to the airport unharmed? Or maybe they're unconcerned with a few more casualties. I don't understand *why* this is happening, why they aren't trying to rid the streets of infection. Has the entire country just gone to pot and they literally don't know what else to do? Maybe things are much worse than I think they are. I wonder how many people are actually left. Imagine if it's just a handful—that would be absolutely insane. It seems the early predictions of 35% of the population being affected by AM13 were way off.

Another point which I seriously hope they've considered is the selection process. I hope they have a plan in place to ensure only healthy people get onto the plane, or things will escalate wildly. From my personal understanding, pretty much every single country has been hit by the virus, so if they really have found a safe haven somewhere, they'll need to be *very* strict to keep it secure. There's so much to think about, and if it's been hastily organised, there's just so much that could go wrong.

What will happen to this country? A big part of me is desperate to stay as far away from any plane as possible. I've never flown before, and a voice in the back of my brain is telling me that climbing into a confined space with a group of strangers spells certain death. The entire time I'm up in the air will be pure torture. Maybe I should just stay here while they sort everything out. If I make this house secure, I'll be okay, won't I? There's food, water, electricity…although I suppose it won't be long until all of that is shut off. I don't know how long I'll last long living in darkness. Oh God, this is such a hard decision.

I keep pacing, flicking between decisions, unsure

of which idea is the right one to follow. I wish I had someone here, someone with a much clearer head, someone more used to making hard decisions than I am. I'm no good alone.

Then a thought stops me in my tracks. What if they decide to bomb the place? It's a sure fire way of killing off all the infected, a good way of preventing the virus from wiping out humanity. Maybe when they want us to move, they mean that to be permanent. My eyebrows shoot up in shock, my chest starts thumping. I'm not ready for this, any of it. Yesterday was all false bravado. I did what I had to do to survive. But this? This change is a whole different ball game. This is too much.

They can't do that, can they? They can't just get rid of an entire island without a second thought, can they? This is our home, our lives. I know it's currently in a bad way, but we could rebuild, go back normal. Or at least, similar to the way things were before.

The Internet. I need to get online to find out more. If I can log on, I might be able to find others still alive, see if anyone I know has survived. If I can find out what others are doing, I'll be able to make a more informed decision. A computer. There must be one around here; everyone has a one, it's impossible to survive without one in this day and age. In fact, I probably saw one yesterday during my search.

* * *

I tap my feet anxiously waiting for the laptop

screen to load up. Why does this always seem to take forever? Especially now. Can't it sense that I need it to work quicker? Can't it feel the impatience seeping out through my fingertips that are poised over the keyboard?

After what feels like a lifetime, it finally finishes loading and is ready for me to actually do something. I click onto the Internet icon, nervously anticipating what I might find on the mysterious World Wide Web. I don't know why I didn't do this before. The Lockdown would have been so much more bearable with social networking, but for some reason, it never even crossed my mind to try it.

Nothing.

The screen stays blank. It hasn't connected at all. I pull at the Ethernet cable, which is plugged into the router. I can't see any immediate reason why it wouldn't connect, it all seems fine to me. Could it have somehow been shut off already? My heart sinks—that's terrible news. I didn't realise exactly *how* much I actually had riding on finding someone, until the possibility crashes down around me.

Now what?

I delicately shut the laptop, stunned. I'm alone. I'm completely and utterly by myself. The only choice I have available to me is to go to the airport. I look around the room of the house I was planning to call home for the time being, mentally saying goodbye to the place. I'll always regret it if I stay here, taking the cowardly way out. I've already faced this awful outside world; I know I *can* do it. I can take supplies with me this time, I'll be more prepared. I just need to push this hollow, sorrowful feeling aside and get on with it. Power through. Who knows, it might be the best decision I ever make.

CHAPTER 4

ALYSSA

"God damn zombies. Why won't you just piss off?" I'm leant out of my bedroom window, screaming at a bunch of undead idiots, and a small part of me is wondering why they won't just do as I ask them and leave me alone. It's so annoying. I've decided now that I want to move on, I don't want to sit in this house with the corpse of my little sister for another minute. I can't stand it; I want to be as far away from her as possible. I'm sure I could even help with the 'clean up' operation that the government has so obviously failed at. I have the right skills and knowledge, I'm sure that's something I'd be great at.

Well, one at a time. This massive horde is a little out of my skill range at the moment!

I just need to get out there. I'm ready. I'm even wearing the perfect outfit for the apocalypse—I look a little like Lara Croft, only with black skinny jeans instead of hot pants. As I put these clothes on,

I imagined I was in a film. I think that's the best way for me to survive, actually—pretending to be an actress. I'm a huge fan of horror films, and I've always pictured myself in them, so now I can actually live out that fantasy. Mum always used to call me her little dreamer, so maybe I should take that to heart and live in my own little world. It'll sure as hell be better than the real one.

I suddenly realise that I need to pull my long auburn hair into a ponytail. I don't normally style my hair this way because it makes my rosy cheeks more obvious, but women are so often grabbed by their hair in zombie films—that's the sort of knowledge that will help me survive. I scan my memory for more tidbits like this, more tips. I knew reading and watching movies wasn't a waste of time.

Duct tape!

If I wrap duct tape around my arms, it'll prevent a bite from piercing through and hitting my skin. It isn't foolproof, but it's a great start. I rush downstairs and scrabble through the kitchen cupboards until I find a roll. I sit down at the dining table to start wrapping, and I find my eyes drawn towards the radio.

The radio that my dad spent the entire Lockdown with. I got annoyed with him, especially when the news became simple repeats. Why couldn't he just have it on in the background and spend some time with us? He was a workaholic before all of this, so I don't think he knew *how* to just sit and talk with his family. Then, as if from nowhere, he happened upon the completely irrational decision to go out on a food run because the deliveries from the armed forced had stopped coming. Of course, my mother insisted on going with him, she wasn't going to let him go out there by himself! It seemed she placed protecting him over her own children—a decision I will *never* be able to get my head around.

I can't work out what my dad's plan was, either. It had only been five days since our last food parcel, why couldn't he have just waited? It wasn't as if we were completely starving or anything. And why did they *both* have to go? I screamed and yelled at them, told them they were making an idiotic decision, that they didn't have what it takes to survive. They didn't know anything about fighting off a zombie, not like me. To be honest, I said a lot of things to them that I now regret.

Of course, they never came back. I knew they wouldn't. I bet they didn't even make it to the end of the street before getting infected. They left me in charge of their eight-year-old child while they went out on a fool's errand and got themselves killed.

Well, I'm glad.

I'm not bitter—not anymore. Anyone who's stupid enough to go out there without the ability to defend themselves doesn't deserve to live. I've gotten past the stage of being desperate, sad, and even angry. I've just accepted it. They weren't thinking of me when they died, so I'm not going to waste any more time thinking of them. I'm keeping stoic—at least I have no one left to love. Caring puts you in danger, the ones that live to the end of the film are the ones who have already lost everything and only have themselves to worry about. I already fit that role perfectly.

Now all I need to do is move, but I can't do it while there's a huge crowd gathered outside. I knew that noisy outbreak earlier was a mistake. I'm not going to end up dead myself. If I stay calm and focused, finding the perfect moment to go won't be too difficult. As I wait, I idly switch the radio on, pleased by the familiar sound filling the room. Actually, I can see how easy it was for Dad to get obsessed by listening to it, without it everything is far too tense and quiet.

CHAPTER 5

ETHAN

I'm very nervous out on the streets now. The infected seem far more active and in higher numbers. I keep thinking this must be because we've all stopped hiding away and we're now out in the open, trying to get to the airport. I'm bound to stumble across someone soon, surely—we're all heading the same way, after all. I hope I do, I would feel a *lot* more comfortable with someone to watch my back. I keep sporadically spinning around, panicking, certain that I hear noises behind me, even though no one's there. It's daft really. If an infected has managed to get that close to me, it'll kill me. And if it doesn't, the shock will more than likely finish me off. I'm really not the sort of person who can do well in this sort of stressful situation. In fact, it's a surprise that I have managed to keep myself hidden and alive for this long.

It *is* better being out here with a purpose, wandering around aimlessly was actually really hard work. I've always lived my life by to-do lists, so having no plan was a real challenge for me. Luckily my destination isn't too far out of town, so hopefully it shouldn't take me too much longer to get there. I'm uneasy and eager to meet up with all the remaining survivors—which is unusual, because I'm normally such an introverted person. I have to keep telling myself that being with a big group gives me a much better chance at surviving than being by myself. I can hide amongst others, I can rely on people. I'm not a fighter so there's no way they'll make me battle.

I'm trying desperately to ignore the little voice in my head, the sensation in my stomach that's telling me this is all a mistake. That it'll never work. That I somehow misheard the plan, or that the airport will be full to the brim of infected. That once I'm in, I'll never escape. I can't stop these thoughts from spinning around my brain, however much I try. I can't stop seeing images of the virus worming its way past my skin and into my organs. I can't bear it. It's making my skin clammy. I can almost feel it. I can almost taste it.

I can't do this right now; I've got to ignore it all. I need to focus. One task at a time. If I just concentrate on each step individually, it isn't so taxing. Don't think about the bigger picture.

I *can* hear them, I'm constantly aware of the sounds around me. The moaning, the growling. But as long as it stays in the distance, I'll be fine. As long as I push it to the back of my brain, I won't start panicking. I still can't get my head around the fact that a disease has affected people in this way.

It's so strange, it isn't right at all. I think there must be a lot more to it than meets the eye, things like this don't just *happen*. I wish I knew why, what has caused it. It's driving me nuts not being in the know. I realise I can get fixated with germs and things, but surely *everyone* is obsessed with finding out about this one. I can't be the only person feeling this way.

I want to know what killed my family. I try not to think about them too much, for fear of sending myself into a tailspin, but that doesn't mean I don't miss them. I deserve to know why they're all dead. Actually we might be told something substantial at the airport. The government must have some answers for us, surely? They've had plenty of time to figure things out. This thought fills me with the determination to continue. If I get there, I'll again be rewarded for my bravery.

CHAPTER 6

ALYSSA

I wasn't listening at first; I was too wrapped up in my own thoughts. It took a while for my brain to latch on to the fact that the rolling news report wasn't one I'd heard before. There was actually something different being reported, a new plan.

"Everyone, please get to your local airport as quickly as possible. There you will be given further instructions and be taken to a safe destination. I repeat, everyone..."

So, of course, my desire to leave has become even more desperate. Now I actually *need* to go. I'm not entirely sure what's going on. I guess in the days the radio was switched off, I must have missed something. To be honest I don't really care about that, I finally have a mission. It's better than just heading outside to kill everyone and anyone in sight. I can only assume the government is setting up refugee camps somewhere, that's the next logical step, after all. At any rate, I'm absolutely fed up with staring at the same four walls and I'm looking forward to whatever is to come. It'll be an adventure. It also makes me feel a lot better, knowing I'll be meeting up with others. It'll be interesting to see what sort of people have made it this far. Who else has got the brains and the guts to survive this much.

I check through my rucksack again, ensuring I have enough supplies to last me the few days it'll take me to get to the airport. I can't take too much because I don't want to have a really heavy bag. I'm sure we'll all be looked after in the camp anyway, so I'm not too worried. As long as I keep in mind the 'three rule' I'll be sure to have everything I need.

"So you can survive three hours without shelter, three days without water, and three weeks without food. Okay, so matches, tarpaulin, clothes, my water bottle…"I sift through the items, all the time talking to myself. It might be silly, but I'm still picturing myself as the heroine in a film, and I don't want to come across as stupid. I know what I need to do and I want that to be obvious.

I'll also need something to fight with. That's the one item I'm having trouble finding. I try to think of the resourceful things people use in films, but they all tend to be set in America, where they have access to guns. I don't particularly want to rely on a knife. I'll have one with me, of course, but I learned from the fight with my sister that it allows the zombies to get far too close. Obviously I know I *can* fight well that close, but I want to give myself every chance of survival.

I half-heartedly pick up a hammer. Breaking through a human skull is seriously hard and I'm unconvinced that this is up to the task. I spot some piping and wonder if that could work. It might not be hard enough, but if I could rip off a long enough part, I could use it as a stunning tactic. I could push them further away while I escape. It isn't ideal. I actually want something deadly, I want to be able to make a difference, but right now I think I should just focus on meeting up with everyone else. Anything else can come later.

I roughly tug at the piping and quickly realise that it isn't going anywhere. Frustrated, I kick it hard and instantly regret it. Hopping around on my throbbing toe, I suddenly notice a golf club tucked away in the corner of the room which must have belonged to my dad. I tentatively pick it up and examine it. It's solid, I'll give it that much, and I could use it in the same way as the piping, just to push the zombies further away. If I encounter them in small numbers, this will suffice. Of course, I'm a lot faster than any zombies, so if it comes down to it, I can run like the wind. It might not be perfect, but I'm pushed for time, so I'll just have to use what's available to me.

I shove on my warmest jacket and grab my rucksack. When I'm ready, I stare at myself in the full length mirror by the front door. I look into my dark brown eyes, trying to spot a flicker of fear. I know it's there inside of me, but I don't want it to show. Pouting as I swing the golf club over my shoulder, and posing in different positions, I mentally prepare myself for what I'm going to have to do.

"Come on, Alyssa, it's time to kick some ass!" Even as I say these words, they sound hollow and stupid. The small amount of terror is burning away in the pit of my stomach, but I'm ignoring it. I've already proved to myself that I *can* kill the zombies; I just need to go out there and get myself to the airport. It's simple really, so why I am paused? "Okay, Alyssa, let's just get this done. You may not even need to fight, so try not to think about that. Just get to the airport and all will be fine. There'll be people there, and food. It's got to be better than this, anyway!" This pep talk works a little better. I force the burning rage to fill me up again. With that on my side, I know I can do anything.

I swing the door open, ignoring my pounding heart. I'm angry, I'm furious; I'm seriously pissed off about AM13. Fuck these zombies, they're nothing compared to me. I'm human, I'm not infected, which gives me one hell of an advantage over these undead, shuffling bastards.

I whisper the words "Goodbye, Lexi," and let one more thought of my little sister cross my mind. Not the zombie version, the living version. The one I loved, the one I wanted to protect.

CHAPTER 7

ETHAN

I feel a lot better gripping tightly onto this crowbar. Of course, I have no idea what to do with it, but it's like a comfort blanket all the same. I found it lying on the street, abandoned. I examined it closely for a long time, deliberating over the decision to pick it up. On the one hand, it *is* covered in blood, so I know someone else relied on it as a weapon, which must mean it's a good choice. On the other, it's covered in blood that's tainted with AM13, the one thing I'm trying desperately to avoid. Also, as no one was in the vicinity, I have no idea how useful it actually *was* as a defensive mechanism.

Despite everything inside me screaming against my choice, I picked it up. I didn't want to be left completely vulnerable and if I can just ignore the negative voices inside me, telling me that the virus is dripping off the crowbar, that by simply holding it, I'm turning into one of the infected, I know I'm a lot better off with it. The end I'm actually holding is clean, but my eyes keep drifting up to the top. My chest gets tight and my legs start to feel numb. Then I have to retrain my brain to focus back on one step at a time. I can't get tangled up in fear right now; I'm trying to keep my breaths to a minimum, finding that the more aware I am of my breathing, the more difficult it becomes to do it quietly.

I'm positive the infected are severely increasing in numbers by the minute, unnaturally so. I keep telling myself that they're just attracted to the noise and smell of people outside, but my brain is becoming more and more fixated on the idea that the virus is airborne, and that the decision to bring us all out here has effectively wiped us all out. It feels like simply breathing in the air is sucking in AM13. It's a possibility, isn't it? This virus must have come from somewhere, and for it to spread as rapidly as it has, there must be something unusual about it.

My brain is constantly whirring, trying to find some logical solution, a reasonable answer. I've never been one to just accept things; I need to know all the details behind it. It's why I struggled so much in education. I would become so obsessed with something that I wouldn't be able to concentrate on other lessons. It's also why I always found working such a challenge, I tried monotonous jobs, such as factory line work, I tried jobs that would force me to use my brain. I couldn't succeed in any of them. In the end, I managed to find a job as a personal assistant, which weirdly suited me better than anything else. Focusing on someone else's diary and problems allowed my brain to switch off from myself. In fact, it's that job that changed my life…

It's almost as if my brain was preparing me to re-open and think about the people I'd forced myself to lock away in a box inside my head. My job as a PA for a CEO of a large IT business led to me meeting Clare, who would go on to become my fiancée—for a short time, anyway. My boss was her father, which meant she was often coming in to visit. Although she obviously came from a very wealthy family, she didn't seem like a rich, spoiled brat. She worked very hard at her own job, she didn't swan around in designer clothing, and she was lovely to everyone all the time.

I fell in love immediately, but never thought she would look twice at someone like me, an OCD ridden, uneducated, desperately shy fool. She could've had anyone in the world, so when she asked me out on a date I was crippled with self-doubt and insecurities. In fact, the first two times I didn't even show up. Nerves got the better of me and I spent those evenings stood in my suit in front of the mirror, watching the sweat pour down my forehead and willing my legs to move. Imagine, standing up such a gorgeous girl who was actually interested in me.

Luckily, for some strange reason, she never gave up on me and our romance blossomed. It was never easy and straight forward. I struggled in this brand new realm of which I knew nothing. I found it hard compromising with another person; it forced me to come out of my shell a bit. After I proposed, she moved into my flat, which presented even more challenges. She didn't understand how I ran things—how could she? I can see now how I resented her taking up room in my precious, perfectly organised space. I also knew she could do better than me, and hated living under her shadow. She was a much larger character than I could ever be. Niggles led to arguments, which led to an inevitable split.

This happened only a couple of days before the Lockdown. We were so preoccupied with our own issues that we barely paid any attention to the virus or the news, so as soon as I finally caught wind of it, I become crazed. I only cared about AM13 and the quarantine, which allowed Clare to be forced out of my thoughts. If I didn't think about her, none of what had happened could hurt me. I'm ashamed to say that I didn't even call her.

But now, I'm standing in front of her parents' town house, which I know for a fact she always retires to when she needs space, and all the emotions I've blocked out are flooding back. I'm overwhelmed with sadness; I'm desperate to see her face again. She could be here; she may not have left yet. I could find her and we could muddle through this together. With a task to focus on, our insignificant problems will fade into non-existence. When we get some sort of life back, we can make another go of it. A proper go. I'll never take her for granted or fall out over silly things again. I've already changed so much, I'm sure she'll be able to see that.

I step quietly to the door, my heartbeat in my

ears. I push the door without knocking. It cracks open and her arms fling around my neck.

CHAPTER 8

ALYSSA

"Oh shit!" I quickly slam the door behind me, panting and grabbing hold of my forehead. I just need another minute to prepare myself. It's not that I'm scared or anything, but opening the door just made me see the sheer volume of zombies out there. Facing that many so close-up is a lot different than peering out of my bedroom window at them. They seem…bigger somehow. I mean, I'm not exactly tall anyway, so I've always felt tiny in crowds, and in a group of the infected, that sensation is even less appealing.

I can't just go out there all guns blazing, I need a plan. I've criticised others for getting themselves killed by doing stupid things, I don't intend to follow that same pattern myself. There's just so many of them. I need some sort of distraction, something to take their attention elsewhere. Where is everyone else that's heading to the airport? You'd think the odd one would find the scent of another human to follow, wouldn't you? I wonder what it is about me that makes my scent apparently so delicious.

If only I had a sniper rifle. I bet I'd be good at that, ridding the streets of the zombies from the safety of my own home before going out with barely any left to worry about. No point in getting an idea like that in my head, I suppose. Gun options are never going to be available to me. I don't know how to shoot, anyway. And guns are stupidly loud and you have to have good aim, so maybe I'm better off without one.

I need a practical solution, one that I can actually work with. Maybe I could leave out the back door? I hurry into the kitchen and peep outside. On first glance, it seems a lot clearer. I'll have to make my way through people's gardens, which may involve a lot of fence-jumping, but it's better than the alternative. I grip the end of my golf club tighter, making my move quickly. I don't want to give myself any time to deliberate or second guess myself. Another minute and I might completely talk myself out of this decision. I don't have time for any of that, messing around will get me nowhere.

I creep as quietly as humanly possible, constantly vigilant of everything around me. I try to be aware of my exact location, and where everything is, but it's actually a lot harder than I thought it would be. Trying to notice everything at once takes up a lot of concentration. Maybe I should just focus on myself and what I'm doing. Speed is of the essence here. I don't know how much time I have to get to the airport so I really need to get a move on. I won't stop listening though, that much I *do* have to keep up.

My boots squelch in the mud, making me jump every single time. I keep looking around to check that no one is behind me. My fingertips have gone red with the cold, and I can see my puffs of breath in the icy air. Why did all of this have to happen now? It would have been much easier to deal with in summer—honestly, it's so inconvenient. The cold is just *another* problem I need to deal with on top of everything else. I need to get to the airport today really; I don't want to have to spend a night outside. Freezing to death is not exactly high up on my wish list. It would be a shame to die because of the cold in the zombie apocalypse.

"Shhh!" I whisper to myself, stopping abruptly. A noise. I heard something, I'm sure I did. What was it? Oh God, don't panic. I just need to work out where it was coming from, and then I can see what it was. I'm sure it was just an animal or something. Nothing to worry about. I will my heart to stop thumping so loudly, I can't focus on anything while it's being so loud.

The silence rings out, but I won't be fooled. I refuse to be killed because I didn't follow my instincts. I know for a fact that I heard crunching footsteps coming from somewhere. I'm convinced that they weren't my own. I force myself to replace the fear I'm feeling with excitement. This is what I've spent my life working towards. I've won one battle, I can win another. Plus I'm well protected; my arms feel stiff with all the duct tape covering them. I swing the golf club above my head, imagining how this scene would look on camera.

I continue to walk, but very considerately, my eyes constantly flicking in every direction. It isn't long until I hear it again behind me. I swing around ready. My breath sucks in rapidly, the cold air stinging the back of my throat.

Of all the sights I was expecting to see, this was not it.

CHAPTER 9

ETHAN

Relief floods through me. She's here. We have a second chance at happiness, another opportunity to make our relationship work. The only woman to ever accept me for all my flaws, to love me for my quirks. I've found her and she forgives me for my neglect at such a terrible time. I *will* make it up to her; I'll never do anything so awful again. Just as I'm about to fall happily into her embrace, I take a deep breath in.

Stench. Rot.

It hits me hard, like a thump in the stomach—this isn't Clare happy to see me and pulling me in for some much needed comfort. This is her rife with infection, and desperately clawing for my flesh. A ball fills my throat and I struggle to get air around it. My head starts spinning and my heart bursts from my chest. My fingers and toes tingle with panic, and I grip onto the wall behind me just to keep me upright and steady. Luckily, in a moment of confusion I somehow manage to get away. The entire time is a blur so I have no idea what happened, but I'm racing up the stairs nonetheless.

I need to get away from her. I *need* to get my head together, decide what to do about her. I also need to check my skin to be sure she hasn't gotten anything on me. I don't want us both to be stuck here, in this house, with the infection. Vomit rises through my system and splatters on the ground beneath me. I don't stop running—focusing on finding somewhere to hide. I can hear her, I think she's right behind me.

Soon I find a bathroom, which is the exact room I need, and I slam the door behind me with a resounding bang. I lean my back against the door, breathing heavily, tasting the sick on my breath, which is making me feel ill. A tear splashes onto my cheek as I think about Clare. This loss feels worse than any of the others. This one is *my* fault. If only I'd been more accepting, if only I hadn't ignored her. If she'd stayed with me, she would still be alive. I pound the wooden door behind me in frustration, I don't want to believe it; I can't accept it. Not Clare too. Haven't I been through enough?

Of course, my banging is met with a much louder, more terrifying thump as a response. I need to act quickly—I can't let her get in here or I'll be trapped. I flick the lock closed and push the washing basket up against the door. If she's strong, this won't hold for long so I can't dither. I rush over to the mirror and switch the tap on. The sound of the rushing water soothes me for a second; if I can get my skin washed I'll be able to think straighter.

As I run the warm water over my arms and face, my pulse slows down significantly. Even though I can't actually see anything on me, I can feel it washing away—leaving me and flushing down the drain. I also have to clean my teeth to get rid of the stale smell, and scrub the splatters of bile that hit my shoes on the way up the stairs. I would never have been able to concentrate with all of that filling my brain. Now I'm fresh, I can focus on the bigger problems.

Next I need to get out. I look towards the door, to where Clare is standing, and remember her hiding behind pillows at the scary moments in horror films. How has my kind-hearted, lovely Clare become the villain? She's now the monster I need to escape from. If I wasn't so frightened, I'd be laughing at the absurdity of the situation.

And now I have to kill her.

That thought bursts loudly into my brain in my negative doomsday voice. It's mocking me, laughing at me, enjoying my pain. No, I can't do that. Although I think *I* would rather someone kill me, than leave me in that infected state, but I would never be able to forgive myself if they found a cure and I'd murdered my beautiful Clare for no real reason. No, I'll find another way out of here. No one needs to die today.

I made a stupid move going upstairs, I shouldn't have let panic rule my decisions. Now it's going to be really difficult for me to get out. I glance out of the window, is there a drain pipe I can climb down or something? No, I'm not going to be able to do that. The only way I'll be leaving is through the front door. Now it's just a question of how. The hungry look I saw in Clare's eyes suggested she isn't going to give me up easily.

CHAPTER 10

ALYSSA

There's a man, all scruffy and covered in blood. His clothes are torn and hanging off of his body. He's wild-eyed and sprinting quickly towards me. Is he infected? Maybe he's been homeless during the Lockdown or something. I'm in way better condition than he is, but then I've only just come outside.

I'm frozen to the spot, watching everything progress in slow motion. I can't work out if he's a zombie or not. He's running, which goes against what I've learnt of AM13, but then viruses *can* evolve. I've read plenty of books where that happens, but it's usually caused by something—a nuclear bomb, maybe—and that certainly hasn't happened here. They would have warned us if there was any chance of radiation poisoning, wouldn't they? I seriously hope that doesn't happen. I don't want to suffer that long, agonising death.

So if I assume he's alive, then why the hell is he

gripping tightly onto the hand of a woman who is without a doubt riddled with the disease? Why would anyone pull a zombie along with them as they run? That's what you're supposed to be escaping from.

I'm fascinated by her appearance. Her head is partially caved in, obviously not quite enough to kill her yet, but it still looks pretty horrific. Her mouth is ripped wide open, which makes her growling much louder than any I've heard before. She is dragging a bloody stump behind her, with bones poking out at all angles. Intestines are dangling down under her shirt and clumps of black blood are sporadically falling from her. She looks so much like a stereotypical beaten up, old zombie, just like a Hollywood construct, that she doesn't frighten me at all, despite the fact that she smells appalling. Even though she's completely disgusting, I feel completely desensitised to her. She snaps violently towards the man holding her, but the motion means she can't get close enough to reach him.

Tension grips me as they get closer. I've mentally prepared myself for the possibility of zombie battles, but I didn't expect to be forced to kill someone alive, but if he threatens me with his little 'pet,' I'm going to have to, aren't I? It'll be so much harder fighting someone with the same mental capacity of me, plus this guy is probably some kind of psychopath. Apocalyptic situations are well known for bringing the worst out in people.

I'm going to have to make myself look like a formidable enemy. If he thinks there's a chance I might beat him, he may leave me alone. Or is that just wishful thinking? I grip onto the golf club harder, very aware of its location right above my head, if I'm going to swing, I need to do it at exactly the right moment. I've got to be clever; my reflexes need to be perfect.

As they descend onto me, the golf club starts to slip. My palms are sweating profusely and it's getting harder to keep hold of the metal pole. "Stop it!" I hiss at myself under my breath. "Stop it now, you can do this. No, you *have* to do this. You've got no choice." I click my tongue, a habit I got into to help me concentrate. It's how I got through my GCSE exams last year.

The man and his zombie pass by me in a blur, knocking me backwards, not even acknowledging my existence.

"Hey!" I cry after them involuntarily, causing the man to turn and face me. He doesn't stop moving, not even for a split second, but I can immediately see the pain and fear deep-rooted in his eyes. The woman must be someone important to him, someone he loved and he obviously can't let go. Maybe it was his wife. Either way, it isn't going to end well. Maybe he's running so that no one kills her, or maybe he knows that if he stops for too long, she will kill him.

I want to laugh at his idiocy. He's made a fatal mistake; he's allowing feelings to affect his decisions. That's a sure-fire way to end up shuffling and moaning in amongst the rest of the zombie population. Well, if that's what he wants to do, then so be it. You wouldn't catch me doing anything so stupid.

Suddenly, another sound gets my attention. I turn slowly; just to be faced with the real reason that guy was running.

CHAPTER 11

ETHAN

I lean over the bath tub, trying to ignore the pounding that's getting louder and louder by the second. I need something to lure Clare away from the door, but what? Unless a loud noise blares out or another person appears somewhere, I'm stuck. I'm going to have to fight. I'm going to have to attack my fiancée to keep myself alive. I don't want to hurt her or damage her in anyway. If a miracle cure *does* appear I don't want any of the changes to her to be my fault. She may have memories of me smacking her and then we'll never get back together. I couldn't bear it.

I grab the crowbar, forcing myself to make a move. I've spent my entire life trying to prevent myself from getting ill; I really don't want to die via one of the worst diseases humanity has ever experienced. I just…I can't let that happen.

If I can stun Clare, for even a second, I can run out of that door and not come back until I have some answers. Really I'm doing all of this for her. I'm trying to find out if there is an end to the disease in sight, just for the slight possibility that I might get my beautiful Clare back.

I hold onto the lock and time stands still. I can hear the ticking of a clock very loud, but I don't know where it's coming from. It could just be my own mind. The negative voice in the back of my head, the one that has prevented me from doing so much with my life, starts yelling louder than ever before. *"Go out there and you're going to get infected. Go out there and you'll die. Go out there and you and Clare will eternally be in that horrendous condition."* I shake it away; I don't need this now. I can't be crippled by the demons that have always haunted me. There are more important things at stake here. I've got to push through the barrier and beat it. I've got no other choice. Listening to it has brought me nothing but misery in my life, I need to break out of the vicious cycle that has been tightening its grip on me for as long as I can remember.

I push the door open and she comes flying through it, landing on the floor. I watch her for a second, my heart aching. Her gorgeous blonde hair, usually tied into a neat bouffant, is straggly and full of grime. Her pale skin is dirty and rotten. Her eyes are blank, there is nothing left of her wonderful personality. I no longer recognise anything about the woman I love so dearly. She scrabbles around, trying to get to her feet. Her lack of awareness, her stupidity, hurts most of all. Clare is such an intelligent woman, I know she must despise being like this. I raise the crowbar, ready to do what's right, ready to put her out of her misery, but instead I bring it crashing down onto the toilet seat, smashing it to pieces. The noise grabs her focus and I rush out of the room, slamming the door behind me.

Tears stream out of my eyes and I slump back against the door. The weeping turns into full blown sobbing that causes everything to start aching. I want things to go back to the way they were. Why did AM13 have to come along and wreck absolutely everything? This is beyond awful; it's a nightmare that I can't wake up from. Suddenly a scratching sound shakes me out of my coma. She's already reacting, still trying to get to me. I wish she could recognise me, but it was widely reported that victims would lose their memories quickly once infected. It's absolutely devastating for the love of my life to regard me as a stranger.

Before I get a chance to move, I feel something dripping on my hand. Blood. Her blood. Alarm shoots through me in an unexpected rupture. I hold my hand as far away from my body as I can, sprinting down the stairs.

The sight of a kitchen sinks calms my heart beat slightly. I scrub my skin roughly, until my hand is red, raw, and peeling, but I need to be absolutely certain that every scrap of the blood is gone. I can't bear the thought of that awful illness touching me, even for a second. Especially after seeing it so close up. I only stop scouring when I hear Clare start to move clumsily down the stairs. She has escaped from the bathroom already. I need to get out; I don't want to risk another fight.

I know I won't catch AM13 just by the blood of an infected touching my skin, unless it gets into a previous cut, but I can't afford to take any risks. I don't want to die, not now. I grab my things together, knowing that I need to leave this very second. When I get out of here, I won't stop again until I make it to the airport.

CHAPTER 12

ALYSSA

"Oh crap." A horde. An absolutely massive horde of zombies is slowly heading this way. A larger group than I've ever seen in any film. More than I thought could even exist. It seems to go on as far as the eye can see. I didn't even realise that many people lived in the UK! They're heading towards me, terribly excited at the sight of a living, breathing human. This is *not* something I expected to encounter so quickly in my adventure. In fact, I was hoping to avoid immense groups like this altogether.

They make the few that I spotted out of the front of my house seem like a walk in the park. By now all of those zombies must have joined this group too. Do I have time to run back home and go out the other side? Do I want to risk that? No, I think the only option I have is to sprint faster than I've ever gone before. I'm so glad I made a point of always keeping active; my fitness level should be able to cope with this, no problem.

* * *

My heart is racing in my ears, each breath is painful and my feet feel red raw, but I force myself to keep on going. There were hundreds, possibly thousands of zombies, and realistically I have no true idea of their abilities. Much as I *want* to rely on my knowledge based on what I've seen, read, and researched, I need to keep smart. If I let myself stop, one of them could be right behind me, and that's a risk I just can't take.

I haven't dared to look. Spinning around to see what's going on behind me takes up precious seconds, time that could be the difference between life and death. I can barely feel my body anymore, I can hardly breathe. If I don't stop running soon, I'm going to collapse. I'm mentally trying to prepare to fight, to take on any that may have caught up with me. I'm not going to let any of them eat me. I need to survive.

Luckily, I can still feel a tiny bit of fighting spirit within me, even though I'm totally knackered. I'm the person *most* prepared for this situation; I'm the one who has been careful and sensible. I deserve to be safe in a refugee camp, more than anyone else does. I deserve to live, I've proved myself. I can be a useful asset; the camp *needs* someone like me.

It isn't long before I fall to my knees, unable to move any more. My body is giving up, even if my mind is still willing me to keep on going. I quickly flick my eyes behind me, and to my relief, nothing is there. Taking in deep gasping breaths, I look around at my surroundings, taking everything in. My eyes are shocked at how far I have managed to run, my brain trying to take in everything I must have passed without even noticing. I must have been running at a lightning pace. I've made it. I've actually done it.

The airport is right ahead.

CHAPTER 13

ETHAN

"Just keep moving, Ethan, you can do this." I'm back to giving myself pep talks. Being alone is not suiting me at all. That realisation has hit me much harder since seeing Clare. Now I feel lonelier than ever. No parents, no family, no fiancée. What if everyone I have ever known is infected? What if they never recover? I'll have to start all over again. I'll have to resort back to explaining my condition to everyone I meet. I hate that. I hate finally opening up about my OCD just to be faced with mild panic before their eyes glaze over. People who have never been afflicted don't understand. They assume you should be able to just stop your ticks, that you should just ignore your inner voice. They don't understand how serious and crippling it can be.

No, I need to stop focusing on the future. I just need to concentrate on what's happening right now or I won't have any more days alive to be worried about. Every single sound is making me paranoid. Every shadow is one of them; every breath I take is tainted with their scent.

I'm lightly jogging, trying to keep a steady pace. I want to get to the airport as quickly as possible now. No more messing about. There I can be protected; there'll be armed forces, or police officers—people with sufficient weapons and the ability to protect me, at least. Then I can relax, then every single move won't be filled with dread. The government is bound to have a lot of security this time, especially after all of their previous mistakes. They wouldn't want to drag everyone outside just to get them killed, surely.

As I'm thinking all of this through, I almost miss a vital moaning sound coming from behind me. I swing around at the last second, just to see a man with his disgusting, bloody body shuffling slowly towards me. My lip curls up in revulsion. His cheeks are sunken in, his eyes rolled back into his head; his skin is grey and flaky. He is moaning lustfully, snarling. Having an infected so close to me messes with my mind. My imagination loses control. I feel AM13 filling my veins and blocking off my airways.

Just as he reaches out to claw at me, my senses come flooding back in a rush of trepidation. My reflexes kick in and I bring the crowbar down on his head with an almighty force. It doesn't kill him, or even knock him out, but blood spurts out in every direction. All I did was push him back a few paces, but that's enough for me to make my getaway. It's such a blessing that the infected cannot move fast.

It's the one thing that gives the uninfected the upper edge. It's the only reason we might beat the disease. If they had the ability to run as fast as we do, I think everyone would have succumbed to it already.

I've got to be more careful, it'll be distraction that gets me killed at this rate. At least my doomsday voice didn't keep my feet rooted to the spot, in the way I suspected it might. I actually reacted in a life-saving manner—self-preservation kicked in at exactly the right moment. For once I actually beat out my affliction and I can be proud of myself.

I keep up my faster pace, and soon I can see it in the distance—the airport. There are many bodies surrounding it, I can't tell from here if they're infected or healthy like me, finally reaching their destination, but I don't stop going. I'm here. I'm excited that I'll finally get at least some of the answers I need.

CHAPTER 14

ALYSSA

I'm not exactly walking, not exactly running, either. I'm just trying to move at a quiet, cautious pace. I certainly don't want to attract any more attention to myself. I don't need any more incidents like the horde until I've managed to pull myself together. I'm not myself at the moment, I'm still shaken up. I don't like feeling this way at all, it doesn't suit me. I can't even get control of my body; it's nervously twitching like crazy.

I've never been one to let anxiety get the better of me. Even though we've always moved around a lot because of my dad's job, I never had any trouble making new friends. Lexi was shy and hated it with a passion, but I've never struggled with being assertive, and that helped me rise in the popularity stakes quickly. In fact, we haven't actually lived here for that long, so it's amazing that I know where the airport is.

I'd only just started college. I was studying a

random mix of A-Level subjects that I thought might interest me because I've never enjoyed academic subjects. Photography, Film Studies, and Design. They were all right I suppose, but I don't think I was going to use them when I finally reached real life. I think I was always destined to end up in some tedious, mindless job that I would hate. Not anymore though, now life will never be the same. Now the zombie apocalypse has come along to save me from a life of boredom. At least there's one positive.

I want to try to recapture that feeling of being the heroine in a film. I was coping a lot better when I had that thought constantly in my mind. I shake my head and put on a determined expression. I imagine the cameras are rolling and I'm acting out a scene. Immediately I feel calmer and stronger. I'm Alyssa, I don't get scared.

It'll be great to reach the airport, which I'm getting closer to by the second. I can't wait to start the next part of the adventure. Even though I never let my expression break, I can't help but think I never could've *really* prepared for this. Much as I thought I had, seeing it in reality is a completely different ball game. Learning to fight and survive doesn't prepare you for dealing with a cannibal that is solely focused on eating you. That's its only mission, and you can't exactly reason with a zombie. They're terrifying enemies—worse than I ever thought they could be.

One of the zombies has been heading towards me for a while now. I've been keeping watch on her out of the corner of my eye and now the time has come to take her out. I raise the golf club above my head, trying to keep my cool. I keep moving, waiting for the right moment, and swing with as much brute force as I can muster. She falls to the ground with a splat. I force my legs to keep going, I don't want to stop. I want that moment to be badass, and I think I may have succeeded. I glance back and see her still lying on the ground in a pile of her own filth, scrabbling to get up. I smile to myself; at least I did that right.

I walk up to the terminal, anticipation fizzing through me. I screw my nose up in uncertainty. It seems kind of abandoned here. I didn't expect that at all. I don't know *what* I was thinking would greet me, people guiding us in? Officials waiting outside to let us know the right way to go? Anyway, my perception must be wrong. I shouldn't get ahead of myself, working myself up before I'm certain of the truth.

Nerves kick up a gear as I walk forwards. My next escapade is about to be decided. I'm about to find out where we're heading next, what security the refugee camps will have, what life will be like there. I wonder what job I'll be allocated. I hope I land something exciting. I hope it isn't a campsite we're going to be living in. It's far too cold for that, plus I *really* don't like the idea of sleeping in a tent. I'd be much more content inside some sort of building.

I step inside, puzzled by the quiet. What the hell? There's no one else here.

CHAPTER 15

ETHAN

Oh my goodness.

There are *so* many people here. The terminal is jam-packed. As soon as I see the sight of families, elderly, children, babies, teenagers, my heart lifts with hope. A lot more people have survived than I ever thought possible. It's amazing; there really *is* hope for this dire situation we find ourselves in. Maybe the Lockdown was a much better idea than I thought. Without it, I doubt any of these people would still be alive. I wonder how they all managed to get here, undetected—I didn't see a *single* healthy person on my travels.

I push my way through the throngs of the crowd, determined to make it to the front. I need my voice to be heard, now more than ever. I'm so focused on my goal, so happy to have made it this far, the faces of Clare, my parents, my family swimming through my mind, that at first I don't notice.

Sniff.

Sneeze.

Cough.

Splutter.

As soon as I realise what's happening, I can almost see the germs flying through the air, the wetness landing on my face. I can feel it, crawling inside my skin, making its way down my throat. My pores are filling up with the mucus, the bacteria. My stomach is swirling, collecting all the evil bugs, getting nauseous, making me sick.

Panic.

My heart is screaming, beating faster than ever before. My throat is closing rapidly; soon I won't be able to breathe at all. I lose focus with my eyes. I can no longer see. I can't concentrate on any sounds, it's all muffled, overwhelming. If I don't get out of this crowd soon, I'm going to faint. I can't let that happen, I'll be trampled. I'll never survive the feet of all these people.

I shove, trying to move, but everyone keeps pushing back, the crowd control nowhere to be seen. All their fingers touching me, spreading it, forcing AM13 inside me. I turn, every direction worse than the last. Faces looming over me, words being yelled in my direction, a blackness threatening to take me.

I finally break free, out the back of the crowd; returning to where I started. I need to get away from here. There's no *way* I can sit on a plane with these people. There's far too much illness. At least one person is infected here, I can just sense it. If someone succumbs to the virus up in the air, there is no escape. Everyone will die. I'll never make it; I'll never be able to do it. I won't be able to force my feet up the steps and into the cabin.

As a snap decision, I move towards the door, fresh air calling me forwards. Just as I'm about to leave, a clear voice breaks through my thoughts, causing me to pause for just a second. "Now everyone, we can't answer any questions at the moment. We need to ensure everyone gets out of here first, so to keep us all safe, just do as you're told and we will discuss at the other side."

They don't have any answers; the government doesn't know anything yet. What a pointless trip this has been. I continue on, turning my back on them all. I'm finally paying attention to the negative voice again. This time I think it's right.

CHAPTER 16

ALYSSA

I've been sitting here for hours, trying to work out where I went wrong. It can't just be that no one else is here, that isn't possible. The report on the radio—it told me to come here. It said to head to the local airport, that there would be 'further instructions' when I arrived. As far as I understand, this is the only airport for miles. It's quite rural here, so I'm sure this is the main airport for a lot of places. I can't *possibly* be the only survivor. I know I've been quite arrogant about my personal ability to survive; there must be others equal, if not better equipped for this. This isn't logical, even if I *was* the only person left alive, someone from the government would have been here to meet me.

It doesn't make any sense.

Unless, is it possible that I was sat inside my home longer than I first thought? Shocked and paralysed by what happened with Lexi? Maybe more time passed during that period than I realised, maybe the whole thing has had a deeper impact on me that I ever thought possible. If that's the case, then I'm well and truly alone. Everyone else has gone off to some refugee camp somewhere. I wouldn't even know where to begin looking for it.

I can't even begin to contemplate the idea of coping alone. What will I do? It'll just be me. And them.

How long can I fight? It's become like a nightmare I can't wake up from. The concept of a zombie apocalypse seems fun, exciting, a change from real life when you're idly thinking about it. I admit I was always all for it. I thought a life where money, careers, and responsibility no longer mattered would suit me much better. Because I knew my life was destined to be full of failure, I wanted the drastic change to occur. But the reality of being alone, surrounding by flesh-eating monsters, it's just awful. If there's no chance of rescue, of finding the others, I think I'd rather be dead.

I think back to the wild-eyed guy from before. I wonder what he knew, if he *chose* to stay behind with his infected girlfriend. I'd like to see him again to ask him what the fuck is happening, especially if he's the only one around. But then, he's probably already dead by now. There's only so long you can last dangling a zombie off your arm.

I liked having a motive, a mission. I don't know if I'll be as good just wandering about aimlessly, trying to survive. I certainly can't head back home now. That thought is much too depressing. My cocky, positive attitude is waning in the dystopian reality that faces me. It doesn't look like the 'clean up' mission is going to be completed any time soon. By the government or me.

Suddenly a glimpse of white catches my eye. I immediately jump up, on the alert. I scan the room quickly, ragged breaths highlighting my position to any enemies. I walk over to what I saw; I'm shocked and reach down to pick it up.

A note.

CHAPTER 17

Alone

DR. JONES

Acetylcholine Malassimilation 1.3 Report

February 28th

5:35 p.m.

Presently, I have seven specimens to assist me with this report, all displaying the varying symptoms of Acetylcholine Malassimilation 1.3—commonly referred to as the AM13 virus.

The virus is evidently RNA, the capsid is impenetrable, protected by a further layer—or virion. It appears to be caused by Orthomyxoviruses, which is why the early symptoms reflect that of influenza.

All of the specimens have an infected upper respiratory tract, which links to their shivering, coughing, aching. However, I cannot see any evidence that interferon is being released and no antibodies are being created—why? Must look further into this. It's the normal body's reaction.

MDOS is the next step, causing an uncontrolled inflammatory response and in some cases septic shock. Similar to pathophysiology; respiratory failure, hepatic failure, gastrointestinal bleeding, renal failure. Mortality rate at this stage is 100% as the chance of survival diminishes as the number of organs involved increases—in the case of the AM13 virus, all organs are targeted too rapidly for medical intervention to assist. What would normally take at least a week is taking mere hours.

Brain scans of specimens in the third and final stage of the virus display some unusual activity—expected, as the level of brain activity after all organs have shut down should be zero—that I intend to investigate further during my time working on this report.

The neurons' cell bodies have a lot of damage—endoplasmic reticulum, ribosomes, and mitochondria are all affected. Only the nucleus, which contains DNA, appears unharmed. The myelin has been stripped from the axon on the interneurons, leaving all the peripheral nerves unprotected—must find out what effect this will have on the senses in the long run, research ganglia?

The cerebellum appears to have lost the substantia nigra, which allows voluntary movement. Without this, it seems the infected are simply living by their instincts. Explains why their motions are often 'jerky' and uncoordinated.

The hypothalamus and pituitary gland are not working at all, the activity in these areas are completely null. Disregards previous evidence that the specimens are run by the desire to 'eat' human flesh. Have seen this occurring in video evidence however, something I need to look into a lot further—

are there any other viruses with similar conflictions?

The cerebrum is no longer made up of the grey and white matter we are accustomed to seeing, it is almost an entirely black area. This explains items highlighted in previous reports into the virus:

The parietal lobe is no longer processing the somatosensory input—will not feel pain. Evidence of sensory aphasia, specimens cannot understand any languages, and do not speak any, but will make sounds.

The frontal lobe and limbic process which contains thought process, memory, and emotions is another completely black area. Specimens show absolutely no activity here, correlates with all previous understandings of victims of AM13.

The occipital lobe and the temporal lobe are allowing sights to be seen, and sounds to be heard, but they are no longer interpreted in a logical manner.

This report is going to be my main aid in determining the origins of the Acetylcholine

Malassimilation 1.3 virus, how humans are surviving this infection when the victims are technically 'dead,' how the virus is spreading at the pace it is, and a cure.

I've been allocated all the possible resources available to help me complete this task. As we are currently in an undisclosed location, I do not have everything within my reach, but I will continue with what's accessible to me.

I have determined from this initial enquiry that I need to delve a lot deeper into understanding AM13 before I can progress, as I've not been able to submit full findings at this stage.

CHAPTER 18

ALYSSA

"Will you just…give *up*!" I pant as I bring the axe down repeatedly, finally forcing it through the head of an old man. Scratch that—a zombie. I never let myself think of them as people. They are hungry, cannibalistic monsters, nothing more. As soon as you start remembering what they once were, you get distracted. Then you die. It really is that simple.

About a month has passed since I finally made it to the airport, late and alone. A month of surviving by myself, of killing more infected than I ever thought I would have to, of trying desperately to find the refugee camp where everyone else is. I travelled for miles trying to find any signs and clues; you'd think the government would have left directions somewhere, just in case. But nothing. I started to think that maybe everyone was flown somewhere; after all, the meeting place was the airport. I guess that makes sense.

So I was forced to give up, accepting that I was

never going to find anyone. I found myself somewhere safe to hole up. I actually got very lucky and found somewhere amazing—almost as if it was designed for this exact situation. A little B and B, all alone down a country lane. It's brilliant. As it isn't near any shops, it was stocked high with food and water. It's also too far out of the way of any towns for the zombies to have noticed it yet.

Of course, I had the unpleasant task of clearing it out initially. Probably the B and B owners and a couple of guests. It didn't take me long. Luckily they didn't really have much fight left in them and I was full of determination and confidence. The odd zombie, like the old man I just finished off, occasionally ambles down this way. But apart from that, I've been living quite a good life. Considering.

I mean, if I had one complaint, it'd be that it's boring. The electricity cut out pretty quickly when everyone left, along with the water and gas. So with no television to watch, no one to even talk to, it's hard. Each minute feels like an hour, each hour could be a week. The only reading material I have access to is a bunch of religious books, which are way too heavy for me to want to read right now. I don't think this is the ideal situation to have some sort of spiritual enlightenment.

Horror films, sci-fi books, survival television shows. They never show you the incredibly dull side of just getting by. They show all the stress and excitement, which may not be ideal, but this is just…snooze.

I've been waiting for a helicopter to come and rescue me. That's what always happens next, isn't it? In all the things I've watched, the characters always end up being picked up by some sort of military vehicles, just as it seems all hope is lost. I know I'm not quite at that stage yet, but if something doesn't happen soon I'm going to lose my mind.

I suppose realistically, I don't *actually* think I'm going to be rescued; it's just a little daydream of mine to while away the long, boring hours. They probably thought that everyone was saved in the first place. I imagine they assumed no one would be stupid enough to get left behind. Well, they were wrong. I'm here, for one!

I don't even imagine myself as an actress anymore, nothing interesting happens anymore to warrant that.

Another bit of bad news is I'm actually starting to run low on the supplies. I've somehow managed to get through almost everything in the weeks I've been here. I have rationed my food a lot more carefully in recent days, at first I was giving in to a lot of boredom eating; I guess I never assumed I was going to be here this long. So it looks like soon I'm going to have to live out the stereotypical zombie apocalypse fantasy. I'll leave this solitude and try to find a group.

As always, I envision there'll be the jock, the geek, the girly girl, the badass girl—I'd quite like to take that role—and maybe even an older married couple with kids. We'll all put our obvious differences aside to use our combined unique skillset to survive. That's how it always happens, right? Hollywood says so.

Although it's been a very long time since I've seen a single living person, I'm confident of my chances of finding others. I didn't find them before because I was too busy looking for a large encampment. But I already know for a *fact* that other people got left behind too, that I'm not the only one in the UK. Of course, I just have to hope that they're still alive. The man I saw outside my house with his zombie pet girlfriend—not that I particularly want to be around him—and E.

I'm still here, and if you're reading this, it means you are too. I'll come back every day at 7 p.m., so meet me here. E.

The note from the airport. The one that brought me a smidgen of hope in a bleak situation. I went back to the airport for three days, eager to meet E, to have someone alongside me in this new, unusual situation. Just to find myself alone, every single time, so I gave up, dejected. E could've been dead, and I wasn't about to let myself fall to the same fate waiting for this unknown person. But I'm certain there must be others. I cannot be the only one. I don't want to accept that it's just me and the zombies.

Well, anyway, I'm about to find out, aren't I? I already have my bags packed, ready to go. I've collected together the minimal supplies that I have left and tomorrow morning, I head out. Nothing will stop me; I don't have anything to lose anymore.

I actually can't wait. I don't feel scared at all. It's

time to inject some excitement back into my life.

CHAPTER 19

DR. JONES

March 2nd

9:50 a.m.

In all of my reading of every single related medical document I have available to me within my given time frame, I've not been able to find any past research or diseases that display anything similar to Acetylcholine Malassimilation 1.3, which will help me within this report.

In this case, and with my previous knowledge, I cannot see vaccination being the solution. Even the smallest virus cell entering the body will cause full infection; there's been sufficient evidence to support this. I'm also extremely wary of the possibility of a cure. With this much damage to the human body, will victims be able to recover and live full lives again? There is no evidence that it is possible to reanimate an organ that has gone through the entire MDOS process.

The specimens I have in front of me have terrible damage to their bodies. I'm going to list this, plus all of the knowledge I have on them below, so it's all in one place. Locating odd bits of paper is wasting too much time:

1. Julie Parnell, 37, Primary School Chef.

5''9', 61kg, dark blue eyes, cropped brunette hair.

Existing medical condition—Trigeminal Neuralgia.

Husband, two children, and her mother are in the camp.

She is in the latter stages of MDOS. Not dealing with the pain well. Currently a lot of screaming coming from her enclosure. She wasn't coherent from the moment she was brought in. She has numerous knife wounds in her stomach and a broken bone in her arm. I understand there was a big struggle just before she was brought in.

2. Mark Andrews, age unknown—possibly late 50's/early 60's?

6"2', 82kg, blue eyes and blond hair.

No information on existing medical conditions.

Doesn't seem to have any family, can't find many details about him at all. He was brought in off the plane immediately, showing flu symptoms. At first he was communicating on and off—that's when I learnt his name. He progressed quickly through the stages and has been in the final stage for two days now. He has scratched and torn his skin throughout stage two, so has a lot of surface damage, but nothing too serious.

3. Oliver Normans, 20, College Student.

5"7', 68kg, brown eyes, brown hair.

No existing medical conditions.

Parents, three brothers and a large selection of cousins in the camp.

His torso is full of bullet holes, one even piercing through his heart. He was brought in during the third stage of infection, and hasn't changed since. He has been banging away on his glass enclosure every day and night with no let up. He can be riled up easily, but not calmed down. He is missing a leg. It's my understanding that this happened after he got infected, it wasn't a pre-existing condition.

4. Jake Riding, 31, Press Photographer.

5"4', 62kg, green eyes, brown hair.

Existing medical condition—ARLD.

His mother is in the camp. He lost his father and sister just before the Lockdown.

He was brought in during his transition between the first and second stage, which allowed me to obtain a lot of useful data. He was very coherent at first, discussing his experiences with me, despite his condition. He hasn't moved on to the third stage yet, despite being here for five days. It has been a very slow and painful process for him—need to figure out what makes the infection affect him slower? He experiences bursts of rage, during which he does a lot of damage to his body. He has also been clawing at his skin regularly, but this has resulted in a lot more damage than specimen two.

5. Ruby-Ann Eastley, 22, Waitress/Actress.

5''0', 52kg pale blue eyes, long blonde hair.

No existing medical conditions.

Doesn't seem to have any family left, came here with a group of friends.

She has been here for over a week and is still only showing flu-like symptoms. I haven't been able to determine if this is AM13 or just influenza, but I have to keep her here, just to be safe. Despite the incessant questions from her that I cannot answer, she is tired and woozy, but this doesn't determine either way. I want to keep an eye on this one because I think if she does transition, she will be very interesting to watch. No damage to her body as yet—will continue to report if things change.

6. Tyler Williams, 27, Semi-Professional Football Player.

6"1', 70kg, green eyes, light brown hair.

Says in his notes that he's suffered a sports-related knee injury in the recent months.

His younger sister is currently in the camp.

The worst case I currently have. The damage to his body is irreparable. He was brought in during the third stage of infection. His intestines have fallen from a hole in his stomach, three bones are sticking out from his leg. His left leg is at a very uncomfortable angle, but this doesn't appear to cause him any problems. I have seen a noticeable difference within him. He was very aggressive at first, banging on the glass, even talking a little bit—similar to specimen three, but in the last twelve hours, he has quieted down and slumped to the floor. Given up? Condition worsening? Time will only tell.

7. Emma Kenshole, 16, GCSE Student.

5''3', 51kg, dark brown eyes, dark blonde hair.

Her notes suggest she may have suffered from anxiety, but with a large question mark, so this information isn't confirmed.

Her grandmother is in camp.

She is the quietest specimen I currently have. She was brought in during stage one. I don't know if she was coherent or not because she stayed silent. Now in stage two, she looks as if she is suffering the same pain as the others, but she still isn't making any noise. I haven't been able to find out any more information about her. According to the board, her grandmother suffers from mild dementia, so isn't responding well to questioning. I intend to run many more tests on this specimen.

Age seems to have no impact, nor gender or race. Although I've not been given any specific details about race, I can clearly see that skin pigmentation has no impact. Every single specimen has reacted differently to the virus, aside from the basic three stages.

A lot of the damage to the victims of the disease will be a huge challenge to repair. If I find a cure, the hospitals will be full. The medical staff, knowledge, and funds are all scarce. I'm sure this will be an added strain, which may not have a high success rate.

I've come to the conclusion that an antidote is the most obvious solution. I know this may not be the ideal answer, nor is it the original purpose for my findings, but I'm positive that it's the most humane response. If we can save all the current uninfected people from getting the virus, that's a positive step in the right direction.

From my current findings, I can safely assume that the body cannot fight off this virus at any stage, as it has evolved past our bodies' capabilities. Specimens should not be able to progress to the third stage, after all the organs—including the heart—stop functioning, it has always been impossible for a human being to continue moving and living after this has happened, but somehow AM13 has defied all our current understandings of biology.

However, it's notable that there's still minimal brain activity, even in stage three, which is obviously very significant. Some of the victims seem to retain the ability to speak and have memories—for a short time, at least. I need to concentrate on trying to understand the virus, and work out how to eliminate or prevent it, rather than bogging myself down in details and questions I may never be able to answer. There is simply no time for this. Illogical as AM13 may be, it's right here in front of me and that's what I need to grasp.

With that in mind, I have been running some tests with the seven specimens, to determine what motivates them, if it isn't the hunger for human flesh, as previously assumed.

I have given all seven specimens access to different meats, even number five—although the look she gave me suggested that my efforts were pointless. This includes animal meat, flesh from a human that has been *dead for a while, and a more recently deceased human. Only the specimens in stage three showed any real interest, but I've come to some conclusions regardless.*

The results I've drawn from these tests, and from my prior knowledge, is that their main desire and purpose is to spread the AM13 virus. The bug wants to move and grow. The victims want to contaminate others. As one bite appears to infect victims—they immediately start the process of running through the three main stages—specimens will, at least half the time, stop then, moving on to another target. This information does correlate with the brain scans I ran before. If 'hunger' was their main objective, they would continue 'eating' until there was no flesh left on their chosen target.

It appears to me that they can smell the virus running through a person's system, which is why they are only interested in the uninfected. They can also smell the difference between human and animal flesh, live and dead flesh. Although I did not notice any unusual perception in the olfactory or limbic system during the MRI, it is a common phenomenon that loss of one scent heightens others and in this case, it seems smell—and to some extent hearing—is all that has survived AM13.

Of course, this completely negates all of the images we've seen of people being 'eaten' by the infected. My personal opinion is that this is down to a competitive 'pack mentality' often witnessed in the animal world. The instinctive reaction is to assert dominance and strength over others. I cannot test this idea further without live bait, but I feel confident in my personal assessment—at this stage, anyway.

Although nothing I write down in this report can be 100% proven fact, I will stand by everything I note down. To the best of my ability and working with the knowledge I have, my findings are correct.

CHAPTER 20

ALYSSA

I start humming to myself as I walk down the road. It's still cold, but nowhere near as frosty as it was last time I was outside for a long period of time, which can only be a good thing. I'm brimming with positivity as I step along the muddy path. It feels so good to have a purpose again. It beats sitting around waiting for time to pass me by. I've never been still for so long before, it was driving me insane. To be honest, I'm not entirely sure what made me stay for so long.

I'm also a *lot* more confident in my chance of survival with my new fighting tool. Any security I felt with that golf club in my hands was false. It was just my coping mechanism. Realistically I wouldn't have lasted very long if I'd gotten too close to any zombies. I was so unbelievably happy to stumble across this nice shiny new axe in the B and B's shed, completely by accident. What a find! It's sharp, easy to grip, and it pierces through zombies skulls with ease. There was also a rusty old chainsaw lying next to the axe. My eyes lit up when I spotted it, but unfortunately it was out of gas. I'm sure it would've been too loud anyway.

Weirdly, I didn't sleep too well last night. I just couldn't seem to get comfortable, silly really, considering I might not spend a night in such a soft bed for a long time to come. There was simply too much anticipation running through my veins, too many possible future scenarios spinning through my mind. Thinking back on that now, I feel a tiny pit of tension appear in my stomach. I don't *want* to think that I may have left behind the best place I could have wished for. I want to concentrate on what's ahead. I don't want to spoil my good mood with melancholy. I can always return to the B and B anyway, once I've collected some supplies, and hopefully gathered together some people. I won't go back there by myself. I can't deal with that loneliness again. You never know how much you're going to miss people until they're gone. I've always prided myself on self-reliance. I've always been fiercely independent, as we never settled for long. Sure, I had many friends, but I always kept the relationships superficial, I never let anyone in because I knew it wouldn't be long before I would be forced to give them up. I assumed I would do well in this apocalypse alone.

I set off this morning, the second the light burst through the clouds, full of energy and enthusiasm. The weariness is starting to hit me slightly now though. I feel like I've been walking for hours. If it wasn't for the light and dark, I wouldn't even know how many days have passed. I haven't bothered to continually keep up with dates and times since being alone; it's seemed pointless with nothing to look forward to. Christmas could have come and gone for all I know. I try to remember the date that the Lockdown started, but so much has happened since then that I can't recall. I may have even missed my birthday. Actually, that's not possible, my birthday is in August. I'm just being dramatic.

I've been trying to plan a route as I walk, trying to remember where I haven't yet been in my previous searches for the refugee camp. I didn't look in the main town area; I figured there would be too many zombies for the government to set up there. Hopefully the undead bastards have all moved on now, because that's where I'm heading first. I wish I knew the town better, then I might have some idea of a safe place a group could be holed up. I'm finding it impossible to remember the place because I only explored it once or twice. When you've seen as many towns and cities as I have, the memories can easily become jumbled and confused.

I imagine it's unrecognisable to anyone by now. It'll probably resemble the seventh circle of hell. If it looks anything like it smells, it's going to be terrible. I guess with the lack of street cleaning and rubbish removal, it'll have started to look shitty pretty quickly. It's amazing, we've been told for such a long time that humans are having a negative impact on the planet, but this just proves what a good effect we've had.

I do stumble across a few stragglers as I go, but

the odd zombie is nothing to me anymore. Not with my axe. I can just take them out without breaking a sweat. Okay, that might be a *slight* exaggeration, it's still difficult to kill them, but fighting them off is much easier. I don't know if I've become stronger or they're getting weaker. Maybe without a regular food source, they're struggling to carry on. I sometimes wonder what Lexi would think of me now, whether she'd be more inclined to listen to me knowing how well I can defend myself. I feel guilty at the mess I made of killing her zombie, but I was so inexperienced then. I probably unnecessarily prolonged her misery. Despite the fact that her turning was her own doing, I could have ended things more pleasantly for her.

Eventually, after what feels like forever, I arrive at the peak of a hill which overlooks the town. I am stunned, frozen by the sight before me. Nerves tingle in my fingers as I drink everything in. It's hard to imagine humans ever inhabited this place. It's more of a deteriorating mess than I could have predicted. Has it really been that long since normal life prevailed? I try to think back over time, but every memory has become infected with the virus. I can no longer picture a time when zombies didn't rule the world.

Smashed windows lie in the road, litter fills the streets, and the remains of dead bodies are on almost every street corner, swarming with flies. Rats scurry in and out of drains, picking meat off the odd carcass as they pass. A smoggy stench fills the air; I can almost see the cartoon green lines wafting from the buildings. It's a ghost town.

There are still a few zombies loitering about, but the town definitely isn't overrun as I expected to find it. Most of the infected that remain are very slow moving, or completely still. I look with astonishment at the ones that have slumped to the ground. They look like they've just given up. Maybe without the scent of flesh to motivate them, there's no point in them moving. It's such a weird and unnerving sight. I find myself wishing I'd thought to carry a camera with me at all times. The stories a photograph of this scene would tell would blow the minds of future generations. It'd show them what life in the zombie apocalypse was really like. If there is any future generation, of course. This could be life forever now, who knows.

Suddenly, a rabble of movement grabs my attention. My eyes were so transfixed on the initial view that I didn't take stock immediately. Six or seven zombies are growling and hammering against a church door. They are desperate, lustful, which can only mean one thing—people. My heart lifts and starts trouncing away happily. It looks like I've found my first port of call already. It's not going to be easy to get there, of course, but I've lived a boring life for too long. Now I'm going to have to use my brain and fighting skills, just as I trained myself to do. I'm going to have to be so careful though. As soon as the zombies catch wind of me, I assume they'll all wake up. When they realise I'm in reach, they may never stop.

CHAPTER 21

DR. JONES

March 5th

1:15 p.m.

All of the seven specimens have now transgressed into the third stage of infection. They are now displaying all the symptoms I summarised in the first page of this report. Although the infection rates may have been varied and at different paces, the end result is always the same. Even the ones that begin the third stage of infection with an element of humanity end up as empty vessels. This is disappointing; I wish I could've learned more from them all.

I've been testing the pain levels as the

specimens transitioned from stage two to stage three, and they were off the charts. By my knowledge, humans shouldn't be able to withstand that level of pain; it goes far beyond the expected threshold—even worse than that of childbirth. Maybe this goes some way to explaining why the parietal lobe is damaged?

Specimen five has not moved at all since entering the third stage of infection. Maybe this process has been too much on her body and the brain activity has not been able to keep up. I cannot determine for certain if this specimen is dead at this point. If she has died, it will take my research in a whole new direction. I will need to find out why only some people can make it to the final stage. It'll finally be a variation in my results—a tangent to work on.

I intend to run detailed blood tests on all seven specimens today, see what I can find out from this. To do this safely I will need the assistance of two soldiers. I'm currently awaiting their arrival. Drawing blood is *going to be a very difficult, dangerous task which I can't do alone. Too many things could go wrong. At this moment, I'm uncertain if any sedatives will work on the infected as their systems don't seem to react to things in the expected way—I may test this today if I'm given enough time.*

I have a theory about one of the questions that I have been given to look at. It's more than a theory, I'm certain it's correct but without proof I have to word it in this way.

Why must the victims be shot in the head to die?

Well, when people are normally shot in the chest, their heart stops beating. When they're shot in another place on their body—say the stomach—more often than not they bleed out. None of this applies to the infected. Their hearts aren't beating to begin with, their blood isn't flowing. The only active function they have is in their lower brain. When this is severed, they cannot carry on.

6:35 p.m.

Notes from the blood tests:

I am not able to determine blood types from the samples I've taken, so I have to assume I have a range of A, B, AB and O. None of the tests show any variety in results, which could be affected by type, so luckily this information isn't vital.

As previously determined, without the heart functioning, blood is not pumping around the body. The arteries, capillaries, and veins are useless. The blood is stationary, causing the plasma to coagulate and form clots. Need to find as much information about haematopoiesis as possible and run further tests into the serum.

An uninfected human typically has approximately five litres of blood. The infected have a much smaller amount than this—approx. 2.75litres. This is possible due to the loss through the damage to their bodies or because they no longer appear to need it to function. I may return to this at a later date, for now I think I can continue successfully without this data.

The virus has consumed all of the white blood cells—neutrophiles, eosinophiles, basophiles, and monocytes, explaining the lack of antibodies, and has latched itself onto the red blood cells at the reticulocyte stage. This allows it to travel around the body at a rapid pace—may go some way to help answer why people are affected at different rates. The ratio of RBCs to WBCs is much higher than normal—2,800 to 1.

Also notable: haemoglobin is absent.

9:45 p.m.

Specimen five, who was previously showing no signs of life, has now made a full turn and is up behaving in the same way as the others. In fact, she's probably the most rabid of them all. By removing her from her enclosure and having her breathe in the scent of the uninfected, I've 'woken her up,' so to speak. I almost wish I hadn't, it's far too noisy to concentrate now. She hasn't shut up once.

The soldiers told me a few noteworthy tales while they were here, of some of the infected that they've had experiences with. They've witnessed, with their own eyes, some function in the same way as the specimens I have, with all their limbs removed, their insides trailing behind them. It seems that no amount of damage to the victims' bodies is enough to even slow them down. I just wanted to write that down so it isn't forgotten. I think there's something very important there. I'm certain it's something I'll return to at some point.

They also told me that they've been instructed to retrieve me some new specimens in varying stages of infection to help me progress with my studies. I read between the lines and have concluded that someone in power is unhappy with my current level of progress. Despite this, I'll be glad to have some new specimens to work with. I don't think I can learn much more from the current seven now that they're in the final stage.

I don't think the board is fully aware of what a challenge they've set me. I'm running dangerous tests, with no prior knowledge in this specific area, all by myself. This isn't even my personal area of expertise. They would be better off with a virologist.

And the worst part of it is none of it makes any damn sense!

CHAPTER 22

ALYSSA

I'm starting to get really fed up and annoyed with my situation. I keep thinking back to how things were at the B and B with regret. Why did I succumb to boredom there? There's so much I could've been doing, if I'd really thought about it. I got so lazy. I wasted so much time bitterly wanting to be out, experiencing more of the zombie apocalypse. How naïve. At least I didn't leave until I was forced to. I'd be banging my head against a brick wall by now if I'd made this mistake any earlier. It was such a better quality of life. Memories of the home comforts of warm sheets, comfy chairs, and plush carpets beneath my feet almost brought tears to my eyes.

To think I was actually glad to be forced out, to have run out of food. Now I'm bloody starving, I haven't slept for days, and I'm no closer to the church. There are people inside that building though, I'm sure of it. I become more certain every passing moment. I can't think of any other reason why the zombies would hang around outside without moving for days on end. Whoever is in there is quite smart, though. They must be being quiet to ensure the crowd doesn't grow bigger. I wonder why they haven't done anything to dispel it yet. It must be rough living with that racket going on outside. I'm surprised that I haven't seen anyone yet; don't they need to go on supply runs or something? I wouldn't have thought that a church is prepared for this sort of situation.

I've spent the last three days desperately trying to get to the middle of the town where my destination lays, but with no luck. I think hunger and fatigue could be affecting my decisions and reflexes. I've tried getting there a number of different ways, but everything seems to be against me. I seem to run into a wall of zombies on every street corner. I return to the top of this hill each day as the light begins to fade because I don't fancy my chances out there in the dark. I'm at a massive disadvantage then because I struggle with my vision, whereas the zombies just carry on as normal. Their eyes obviously no longer work in the same way as ours. I didn't need to research that, it's obvious from their behaviour.

I sit every night, shivering violently in the icy breeze. I'm far too frightened to go to sleep; I'm not ashamed to admit that. I hate being exposed and vulnerable. I can't relax without four walls to protect me. I feel like I could start hallucinating soon I'm that tired now, but then again that could just be my dramatic flair speaking. I'm not going to last much longer if I carry on this way. I really don't want to die in such a meaningless, pathetic way. If I *have* to go, I'd much prefer it to be in a blaze of glory—not just because I was a little knackered.

As I try to plan the route for tomorrow, I can't help but notice again that from up here, the roaming zombies seem scarce. When I get in the midst of it though, it's a whole different story. I don't know if that's my perception or if they get excited by my scent and appear from every nook and cranny. Either way, I'm going to have to find a way around it soon. I pass the dark hours away, trying to plan. Always planning, that's what I said, right? Always planning is the key to survival.

All I really want to think about is the people inside the church. I want to meet them so badly. In my darker moments, I tell myself that I'm so desperate to see an alive face that I'm inventing a mission to complete, I'm imagining people to give me something to do. But of course, that's just me being negative, so I always force these thoughts to one side. When I actually meet these people, I bet they'll be so surprised about everything I've been through to get to them. I wonder if they'll have stories anywhere near as interesting as mine.

The one good thing to come out of this constant battling with zombies is that my fighting skills have improved immensely. There's no way the group could reject me, I think I'll be a brilliant asset. I don't think anyone would *really* be cruel enough to leave me out in the cold in this situation anyway. That's just another concept that I've seen in films that I'm trying to apply to my real life.

I wait anxiously for the light to start streaming through the clouds and start moving the second it does. I'm stiff for my first few steps because of the ball I've spent the last few hours curled up in, trying to keep in body heat, but I'm building myself up to be full of determination. I need to be strong today; I need to get through it. I've got to get into that church; I don't want another sleepless night. I can't survive it, I won't. It'll damn near kill me.

As soon as my feet hit the streets, I take off running, praying that the sound of my shoes pumping against the concrete doesn't bring the zombies out from their hiding place too quickly. This is one of the paths I attempted yesterday and I killed a lot along the way, so in theory it should be pretty empty. Of course, that doesn't always work in practice. As I reach a street corner, I pant, pinning myself against a wall, waiting. Listening intently. I peek around the corner quick as possible and the sight before me stops me in my tracks.

Another message. Another note from E, written in what looks like paint, across a wall.

I'm still here. E.

E was here? Why would E be here and not meeting me at the airport like the note promised? I look around, trying to see if anyone is anywhere in sight. Nothing. Whoever it is could be dead by now. Realistically, E *could* be just another zombie. Even so, I can't stop my legs from automatically walking towards the letters. I instinctively reach up to run my fingers over the paint, to allow thoughts of another lonely person surviving this nightmare run through my brain. I wonder what happened for E to get left behind. I wonder if the story behind these notes is similar to mine.

When I look down at my fingers I'm amazed to see them white. This note is new.

CHAPTER 23

ETHAN

I can't stand it. I can't take it for another damn second. This is horrible. Being alone is driving me insane!

Every single day I wish that I'd been brave that day I went to the airport. I know it seemed like a dangerous decision to get on a plane with all of those people, and all of the unknowns at the time—but is *this* really any better?

I keep leaving notes around town, just praying that someone, *anyone* will eventually see one of them and come rescue me from this hell. But nothing. No one. I know I should probably give up and accept that it's just me, but it's too much of a horrifying prospect.

Me and *them*.

That can't be it. I can't be all that's left.

I thought for a while that people may return. That if anyone *did* survive, they might return to England to look for any other survivors, or to cure the infected, or even to have another go at living here. But it seems that I was wrong. It's been such a long time and I haven't seen a single soul.

I spent a short while considering suicide. I can't live in this world; I'm just not strong enough. I remember the day I stood there, a rusty blade in my hand. I ran it along my neck, willing this whole nightmare to be over. I was ready to die. I tried to push it in; I attempted to apply some pressure. That's all I needed to do and I would be free from this hell. But courage never came to me. As desperate as I was to end it all, I wasn't brave enough to even do that. I'm useless. I'm pathetic. I can't do anything right.

So I just keep on going, waiting for something, anything to happen to take the decision out of my hands.

My OCD is definitely getting worse. Before all of this happened, I had been struggling with it, but it had been under control—now, it's slowly becoming all consuming, infecting every single one of my thoughts and actions. It was going to get me killed eventually, I'm sure of it.

I keep finding homes to hide in, just as I did before. There might not be any running water to clean myself with anymore, but I still feel safer inside, with four walls to keep them away from me. Not much safer, but it'll have to do. It isn't like I'm surrounded by options at any rate.

Occasionally, I'll eat. Often, I won't. Usually, I have to be on the brink of starvation before I'll allow myself to do so. These days, my doomsday voice is telling me—screaming at me—that AM13 is everywhere, and it's becoming increasingly difficult to ignore it.

"Don't eat that—that's where the virus is hidden."

"Don't breathe too deeply—AM13 is airborne."

"Don't touch anything; you'll become infected in a second."

It's actually becoming exhausting to listen to, and it's increasingly getting louder and more insistent. I'm finding myself heading towards a place where I'll be too afraid to even move. I know what it is, and I wish desperately that I could accept it for what it is and ignore what it's telling me, but I just *can't*. I've tried, I really have, but it gets me every damn time.

Really, all I want to do now is go back to Clare. I want to be with her. That's what I'm currently working towards, but I don't know how long it's going to take me to get there. It's a situation that ends in certain death, which is why it's going to take a whole lot for me to act upon my wish. For a coward, considering it for *real* is damn near impossible. But then again, if I'm going to die anyway, why not do it with the woman I love? And on my own terms at that.

I step into a new home, flickering the lights on and off—even though they don't work anymore. This tick has become intrinsically linked to my one bout of good luck, and now I can't do without it.

On, off.

On, off.

On, off.

Then, instead of instantly racing from room to

room, like I know I should, I sit quietly, peering out of the window, just waiting for someone to magically appear.

CHAPTER 24

DR. JONES

March 6th

10:50 a.m.

I've just come out of a review meeting with the board members—the people in charge of this whole operation. Two things are now very clear to me. The first is that the writing of this report is absolutely useless. I've tried to keep it as professional as possible for them to read, which has been hard for me because I've always had an assistant to decipher my scruffy notes. They didn't want to see any of my work; they weren't interested in any of my progress. All they want are answers, solutions. I can understand why, I suppose—this is a desperate situation. But I have to do it this way; the process must be completed for a sensible conclusion to be drawn. This is how I've always worked; this is how I was trained. Answers don't just jump out from mid-air.

One of the men—the sneering one, I'm not sure of his name—suggested that I keep on making my 'little notes' for the next scientist to come and take over my work. He winked at me, making me feel sick to my stomach. This is when the second realisation hit.

I'm not going to make it out of here alive. If I don't solve this soon, they're actually going to kill me. They didn't say that, of course, but I'm smart enough to recognise when I'm being threatened. I have no idea what these men are really capable of—society is currently abiding a new set of rules. One where human rights aren't considered. That's terrifying.

I begged to see my family. After all I'm

doing, you'd think this simple request would be met. But no, they might become a 'distraction to my work.' Surely it's more distracting not knowing if they're okay? They just want another thing to dangle over my head. If I'm going to die down here, I want to at least be able to say goodbye to my wife and child. That's fair, isn't it?

I'm far too angry at everything and everyone at the moment, so instead of continuing with my research, I'm going to write down my experience here. All of it. Maybe as a warning for the next person that comes along. Or maybe so my legacy is complete. I don't know why, but I feel like this is something I need to do.

For me, it all really began only a few days ago, although it feels like a different lifetime now. The Lockdown was quite obviously failing; it didn't take a genius to work that out. The number of infected on the streets was increasing rapidly, almost by the minute.

I was scared, I'm sure we all were.

I had made a decision, just before the Lockdown. One that would come to haunt me the entire time I was quarantined inside my home. I decided to shun work and spend the time with my family. I knew I wouldn't be missed; I was hardly the most talented or the most experienced scientist in my laboratory. At twenty-nine, I'm still considered very young in my field. I'm a microbiologist, so although I know about disease, it isn't my specific area of proficiency. There were many virologists working on AM13, so what use could I possibly be? I didn't think my level of knowledge could bring anything innovative to the plate, so I chose to let the bigwigs take control.

I spent every waking moment listening to the news and worrying about their lack of progress. Was I wasting my talent by not working? My wife, Ashley, and my five-year-old daughter, Melody, were glad I was with them, of course. They relished the time with me. It did make me realise how much time I actually spent away from them normally. I've felt a lot of guilt about that ever since—just another burden on my shoulders. Then the announcement came. Everything had broken down, fallen apart, and we were to get to the nearest airport as soon as possible.

I guess that during this time, if I hadn't been with my family, they wouldn't have survived. At least I'll always have that to be grateful for, whatever bad decisions I made.

As we stumbled into the airport, exhausted and stressed after having a few near misses, we were ready to breathe a sigh of relief. But things didn't stop there. I was immediately taken aside by a government official. He told me with great vigour and enthusiasm that I'd been handpicked to join the medical staff working on a cure. I was so pleased—finally a chance to make up for my mistake, an opportunity to help—that I didn't even think it through. I was happy, can you believe that? To make things even more tempting, he told me that if I was happy to comply, my family would be taken really good care of for the rest of our lives *wink wink*.

Who could refuse an offer like that? I should have, of course; it was far too good to be true.

I tried to explain the importance of this project to Ashley, but she became distressed and hysterical. I couldn't make her understand that I was doing this for her, for everyone. That I was doing it to get rid of AM13. I think she just saw it as abandonment. Regardless, I was forced to say a quick goodbye before we went our separate ways. She got on the plane with everyone else while I waited behind to get on a different flight. Of course I was upset by her reaction, but I was more pleased that I'd been 'handpicked' for my skills.

Before boarding, I was inexplicably blindfolded. I didn't question it at the time, assuming there was a valid secrecy reason for this. I was ushered into my seat, where I became increasingly confused, nervous, and excited in equal measures. Someone told me not to remove my blindfold until given explicit permission, but curiosity got the better of me and I peeked.

I was stunned to find myself sitting completely and utterly alone in the economy section of the plane. I could hear muffled voices coming from behind the curtain, in the first class section. It seemed I was the only one not travelling in luxury. Where were all the other great scientific brains and doctors on this so called assembled team?

Turned out there wasn't any because, of course here I am, completely and utterly alone.

I wasn't officially allowed to see again until long after we had landed, so I actually have no idea where we are. By the flight length, I am going to guess somewhere in Europe, but I could be wrong. I was taken into my laboratory, shrouded in secrecy and whispering. I asked repeatedly why there was no one else here with me working on this completely alien disease. No answers, not really. Just that I'm the best available.

That's not what I wanted to hear, not at all.

Does that mean all the other scientists have died? Got infected? What about all the guys from my workplace? Did none of them survive? Of course, even now no one will tell me anything, but I can't stop these questions from whirling around in my mind constantly. Am I really the best left? If so, who do they think is going to follow me? That was probably just empty threats. Even so, this responsibility is such a hard one to shoulder.

Actually, on that note, I think I will try to keep this report detailed, even if it is just for the scientist who follows me. Then, if anything does happen to me, my work won't be wasted and the next person won't have to start from scratch—especially if it's someone more inexperienced than I am.

Here I'm going to describe the laboratory, just because I feel like I should. It may add to the understanding of my work. This room seems to have been purpose built for this exact scenario. Of course, that can't really be true, there hasn't been enough time to develop anything like this, but to be honest I'd rather not know what went on here beforehand. The possibilities are endless and frightening.

It's small. That is the most notable thing. It is a fairly small room, with no window. But then that's probably a good thing, because sunlight can affect results. There are eleven individual enclosures surrounded by bullet-proof glass. These are where the specimens are being kept. These are tiny. I feel terribly sorry for the people who were brought in during stage one of the infection. I felt awful staring at their confused faces inside these 'cages,' which have barely enough room to move about in. It's undignified.

There's an adjoining room, which is just as small, containing a very uncomfortable camp bed, the MRI machine, a toilet, and a shower. I only have running water for an hour a day, so getting an ice cold shower has become a real task. Timekeeping is just not my thing. Very cramped conditions, but I'm not exactly here to live the life of luxury.

This is also the room which contains my desk. It's messy, of course, with bits of paperwork scattered everywhere, but it's organised chaos. I keep this report on this table—the only thing I've treated very carefully.

So anyway, that's where things stand at the moment. I think next time I see the board I'm going to ask them to attempt to locate other scientists from other countries. They can't honestly expect me to believe that I'm now the only living person with any scientific knowledge left? If they want me to find an answer to AM13, I'm going to need help.

If I'm perfectly honest, I'm terrified that there isn't an answer.

CHAPTER 25

ALYSSA

I'm frozen to the spot, staring at the wet paint on my fingers. E wrote this recently. Very recently, meaning they are still somewhere around here. I wonder if it's one of the people inside the church. It would make a lot of sense, I suppose. I glance around fervently, wondering if E can see me. I wonder if whoever it is, is out there watching me, waiting patiently for my next move. I wave and say a quiet "hello?" hoping for some sort of reaction. If I look friendly enough, I might persuade E to come and get me. I can't speak any louder because it may attract a bunch of zombies. This day hasn't gone too badly yet, I don't really want to change that.

No response. Now what?

I decide to stop acting so carefully, to start taking some serious action. I'm going to ignore the dizzying drowsiness and take this as the kick up the ass that I need. I'm going to use this determination to find someone, anyone today. As E isn't making a magical appearance, I'm going to focus all of my efforts on the church. I force myself to picture the cameras rolling and imagine this as the scene that turns the entire film around. This day is important, probably the most significant so far and I need to be ready for whatever is about to come.

I take a deep breath in, preparing myself for a fight, and start running, faster than I've gone in a very long time. If I can just get myself within sight of the church, I'll be able to get inside. Whoever's there may even help me.

It isn't long before I'm grunting and panting, and sweat is pouring down my forehead, but I'm killing off zombies left, right, and centre without too much trouble. I start to feel badass again, I'm back to feeling like a heroine and I'm relishing this newfound power trip. I start to think that maybe I was designed to survive the zombie apocalypse. That this has been my purpose all along. I certainly feel more suited to this lifestyle. Before, no matter what, I always felt a bit lost and detached from life. I never really cared about anything particularly, I never felt whole. But as I swipe my axe at every undead, disgusting bastard that comes my way, I feel like I matter.

I'm covering myself in blood and grime, I must look disgusting by now, but I don't stop. I can't. The noise my axe makes as it pierces flesh makes my stomach turn, but at the same time, it's oddly satisfying. I pull a piece of intestine from my hair as I watch the head of a young boy roll off and hit me in the feet. I look at his eyes for a second too long and a chill runs up and down my spine. This is worse than any horror film I've ever seen. There's far more gore in real life, it's much more terrifying. Words can't describe the effect undead monsters can have on your mental state. It's rough.

After I've been winding down twisting streets for hours, taking out anything that crosses my path, I finally come face to face with the building I've been aiming for all this time. The church. My heart lifts at the sight and I feel a new wave of energy hit. I've done it; I've succeeded in reaching my goal. After so many days creeping around, missing out on opportune chances, I'm finally here. I can't believe how easy I've found it today, where have I been going so wrong?

Now there's just the matter of the army of hungry zombies hammering away on the door to deal with. I pin my back to a wall while I catch my breath and think. I need to keep out of sight while I plan. I've got to pull them away from the doors while I get inside, without putting myself in too much danger. Maybe the best way to do that is attract their attention, force them to chase me, and then use my speed to circle back around and get inside before they return. So much could go wrong, but no idea will be foolproof.

At the thought of this plan, my heart starts hammering against my chest and my breaths get shorter and louder. It's a risk, of course it is, but I think I'll be able to pull it off. I psyche myself up by imagining how good this would look on the big screen, which goes a way to calming my nerves. I run with my instinct before I can change my mind.

"Hey," I call out, nowhere near loud enough. I

let out an awkward cough and try again. "Hey, you lot, look at me!"

With that, a few of them turn around to face me. I have their attention. I wave my arms above my head, laughing loudly, trying to keep a confident expression on my face. I push the nerves away, focusing on the task at hand. I *wanted* this to happen, this was my aim, I mustn't let fear get in the way of that. "Come on then, come and get me!"

Suddenly something catches my attention in the corner of my eye. A lightning quick movement behind one of the stained glass windows, a glimpse of a person. I was right, there *are* others inside there. Relief floods through me and I realise that everything is going to be all right. I'm not going to be alone any longer. In this moment I can finally admit to myself how terrified I was that I was going to find the building empty. As much as I tried to ignore the negative thoughts, they were always there. Another surge of adrenaline rushes through me, wanting me to speed things up.

"Come on then, you ugly bastards, follow me!" I yell this much louder and with a lot more confidence.

The stench of rot wafts towards me as the zombies begin to shuffle. Finally, my plan is getting into action. I wait, tension filling every pore. I need to let them get close enough to me that their interest is piqued. I don't want them to turn back again as soon as I sprint off.

"Come on, come on," I murmur, tapping my foot anxiously. Where my body is screaming at me to run, my brain knows I need to stay put for just a little while longer. I suck in a deep breath, unsure of how much more of this tension I can stand.

Come on. That's right, just a little closer. And go.

I pump my legs as fast as they can move; running around the building, shouting sporadically, just to keep the zombies coming. I'm scared that without the visual, they might forget all about me. For the first time since this all began, I hope my scent is still wafting under their noses. I zigzag through streets, not entirely convinced that I'm going the right way. My breaths are getting shorter and harder to take, how many corners do I have to turn before I find this damn church?

Before I know it, I'm there. The door is open, keeping me pushing on. I fly through the entrance, collapsing to the ground, but not without noticing that my welcoming committee is the barrel of a cold, metallic gun.

CHAPTER 26

DR. JONES

March 10th

8:55 a.m.

Today I received five new specimens, all from inside the camp and in currently stage one.

8. Kain Curtis, 14, School Student.

5''1', 68kg, green eyes, brown hair.

He's had his appendix removed.

His mother and sister are in the camp.

He is displaying very severe flu symptoms and appears to be in a lot of pain. I've tried communicating with him but haven't had any response as yet. According to the notes that were brought in with him, he has been in this condition for a few days now.

9. Toby Pickering, 47, Driver.

6"4', 72kg, blue eyes, light brown hair.

No existing medical conditions.

His father is still in the camp.

According to everything I've seen up until this point, he will be in stage two very soon. He's delirious, but I've still succeeded in having the odd conversation with him. During the times when he is coherent, he doesn't sound ill at all. If it wasn't for his pale, sweaty exterior, I may suspect that he's recovering.

10. Rhys Thomson, 26, Graphic Designer.

5"7', 59kg, pale blue eyes, blonde hair.

Has an existing medical condition— asthma.

No family left in camp.

He describes his own condition as 'the sniffles.' He keeps telling me that he's heard rumours about what's happening down here. I don't know what he means by that, but I can summarise that it isn't positive. I haven't considered life outside these four walls since

I've been here, apart from my family, but his comments have got me thinking. I've tried questioning, but it's clear that he doesn't trust me, so he isn't telling me anything. I'm haven't determined yet if this specimen is actually infected with AM13. But then, I did think the same about specimen five and she has now fully succumbed to stage three.

11. Alex Hodgkins, 19, University Student.

5"7', 61kg, blue eyes, blonde hair.

No existing medical conditions.

Eden Hodgkins—another specimen—is his twin, their parents are both still in camp.

These twins are both clearly infected with AM13. It's affecting their appearance already and they're only in stage one. By just looking at them you'd assume that they're well within stage three: pale, greying skin, pus filled spots around their mouths. Despite this, they're both fully coherent, talking only to each other, offering comfort and discussing their parents and past lives. Neither have been responsive to me.

12. Eden Hodgkins, 19, Singer.

5''7', 60kg, blue eyes, blonde hair.

No existing medical conditions.

Alex Hodgkins—another specimen—is her twin, their parents are both still in camp.

*See notes for specimen 11.

Three of the specimens—two, three, and six—were taken away as the new ones were brought in. They had been in the third stage for quite a while now so were no longer deemed 'necessary'...I guess that's a fair assessment. I've realised that once they reach stage three, there isn't a lot else the specimens can teach me. I can only assume that as soon as they leave the laboratory, someone will put a bullet in their brains. Even though I know this is the best way, the only way, I can't help feeling a little sad about this.

I know this is illogical, after all they're probably better off dead than in the condition they're in, but I can't stop thinking about their families out there, probably waiting for them to return cured. Instead,

I've chosen to sentence them to death. I've selected to work on an antidote, rather than a cure. Although my reasons for this are solid, I can't control my emotions. I've never worked with human specimens before and it's much harder than I ever thought it would be. It's difficult not to get attached at all. In fact, in these lonely conditions, it's impossible. They're the closest thing to company I have.

I'm finding it a struggle with the new specimens, because they're all in stage one, they're in the position to ask me some very difficult questions. Especially number ten, Rhys Thompson. He's convinced that he isn't infected and he's continually asking me when I'm going to release him. He won't accept that it isn't my decision, but I really don't have any control around here. I wouldn't be doing things this way if I did.

I don't know what I would be doing, I haven't thought that far—but this isn't it.

At lunch time, the derision became much more intense. I can understand, of course.

The specimens are seen as wasted mouths to feed, so their portions are much smaller than mine. In fact, I always get far more than I can possibly eat—a small part of me is concerned I may actually be putting on weight! I tried to clear the tension by sharing out my food, but I'm still quite obviously immensely disliked.

I'm going to run all of the standard tests on my new specimens; MRI, blood tests, saliva, and urine tests, just to see if I can gain any new information. I don't think I will, except maybe from the twins. There may be something genetic I can pick up on. It's the only hope I have at the moment.

3:40 p.m.

Specimens eight, ten, eleven, and twelve have shown me through the blood tests, that the white blood cells are already being targeted by the AM13 virus, so no antibodies can be produced quick enough to react. Some of their organs are already starting to deteriorate, for example the kidney function is already very low. The blood is starting to thicken. I did notice this in the previous tests, but assumed it was due to the coagulation process.

I didn't pick up anything new from the other tests—just a repetition of information I've already noted. Also, unfortunately, the twins didn't provide anything new, so I can officially rule out genetics as any sort of input. I did suspect as much.

Specimen nine had already reached stage two by the time I ran the tests. I could see from the MRI that all his muscles had tightened considerably as an attempt to protect the body from the pain. This is often seen in victims with, for instance, slipped discs. This has caused his skin to be extremely sensitive to even the slightest touch, so pushing a needle into his veins for the blood tests was pure agony.

5:00 p.m.

This process today has raised more questions in my mind than it has answered. I *want to find out why some people progress through the three stages quicker than others, and why some seem to deteriorate much faster—like the twins. I don't think that the two are linked, i.e. the ones that develop quicker, aren't the ones that deteriorate quicker. This may go some way to finding out how to stop it. There has to be way, I just need to figure out what it is.*

CHAPTER 27

ALYSSA

I glance up, panting heavily, and blink my eyes hard, trying to focus; the light is bearing down on me so all I can see is a blinding white. Also, I may have hit my head during the fall, I'm not entirely sure. All I know is that it hurts like hell. I finally find four curious eyes boring down on me.

"I think she's waking up, Mum!" I try to work out what this young voice means. I didn't pass out, did I? I'm very disoriented, and as much as I try, I can't seem to remember much of anything. I grab onto my forehead, trying to make the pain subside. A nauseating dizziness grabs hold of me, which makes everything else pale into insignificance. I hear footsteps rushing towards me and my hackles immediately rise. As I push myself into a sitting position, my memory comes flooding back.

The gun. The one that's still pointing at me now.

"Where the hell did you get a gun?" I start speaking a long time before my brain and senses kick into gear. I'm just so shocked by the sight—you just never see guns here. But someone has managed to get hold of one, and in the zombie apocalypse too. To me, that's just amazing and *so* smart. I wonder if I'll ever be allowed to use it. That would be awesome! I get distracted for a moment, picturing myself in a black cat suit, my long dark, wavy hair cascading down my back, holding the shotgun...

"What are you doing?" A male voice surprises me, and brings me back down to the harsh reality that I'm actually being threatened with said gun. Didn't that kid say *mum*? I try to focus my eyes on the person who holds my life in his hands. I can just make out his outline in the illuminating light, and his large frame fills me with terror.

I start to stumble over my words. "I was…I was sending the zombies away so I could, um…"I trail off, unsure how to finish that sentence. How do I say "*take me in, please*" to these strangers who are clearly feeling hostile towards me? I'd forgotten how antagonism rears its ugly head quickly in all apocalyptic movies. How stupid of me. They probably think I'm some kind of bandit, here to rob them or something. I try to convey my honesty, my niceness, my innocence through my eyes. Seconds pass, each one feeling like an hour. To my utter relief, the gun eventually lowers and I let out a deep breath that I hadn't even realised I was holding.

"Why d'ya say zombies?" the strange voice scoffs, confusing me immensely. What the hell does this guy mean? Hasn't he seen what's going on outside? This church has windows, for crying out loud, he must have looked out of them at some point. Or heard them moaning, the growling. Or smelt the rotten stench of the air. A million thoughts all run through my brain at once, none of them explaining what on earth this guy could possibly mean with this question.

"The…the zombies. You know, infected with AM13? Roaming the streets? Banging on this door for days?" This entire situation has completely knocked the wind out of my sails. I didn't expect any of this at all. I certainly didn't anticipate my new group to have no idea about zombies—*that* was never in any of my fantasies!

I look up properly now that my eyes have fully adjusted, to take in my surroundings. I'm faced with what appears to be two families. A Hispanic man, holding the shotgun, with his other arm around a young boy who looks exactly like him. They *must* be father and son. Then, on the other side of the room is the aforementioned "mum," another young boy, and a teenage girl, who all have very pale, almost translucent skin, and matching hair that's so blonde, it's almost platinum.

They're all looking at me intently, and I'm sure my expression is the same. We're all regarding each other, trying to figure out where we go from here. I can't help but think that this isn't exactly the group I envisioned myself surviving the rest of the apocalypse with. I don't like to sound awful, but these people look kind of *dull*, and there are far too many children for my liking. I wanted my time to be action packed, not full of parenting. I can't really imagine they're going to make my adventure exciting and fun in any way, and haven't I spent enough time being bored? Maybe I should just turn around and head back outside, hold out for better.

But the thought of going back outside to the starvation and insecurity makes my insides recoil. I guess I'll just have to accept what is here in front of me. I might not survive long enough to find anyone else. There might not *be* anyone else anyway. I need to look at the positives of my situation, I can always transform this group, bring in others to make it what I want. I need to stop thinking such ungrateful, bratty thoughts—at least I'm no longer by myself—that's a much worse prospect.

I break the silence. "Are any of you E?" It's a very high possibility. The message I found today wasn't *that* close to here, but I haven't seen any signs of anyone else. I find myself really hoping that the message writer is here. I grip onto the original note in my pocket, anticipation fizzing. At the moment, E is a bit of an enigma, an unsolved mystery. I won't pretend that it's all I've been thinking about since I left the airport, but the painted message has certainly sparked a brand new interest.

"No." The man shatters my illusion. "I've seen a couple of messages around the town, though. I actually thought it might be you for a minute."

Full of disappointment and exhaustion, I sigh. Unfortunately I can't sleep yet, however desperate my body is to give in. I need to get these people to trust me first. They'll have to accept me into their group before I can be cheeky enough to ask for a bed for the night. If I'm *really* lucky, I might even get food.

To hurry this process along, I speedily launch into my story of my time during the apocalypse. I may edit it slightly to make it more satisfying for myself, but the basic details are the truth. This works in exactly the way I wanted it to, because it isn't long before they're also opening up to me. Thankfully, their tales are accompanied by dinner.

Randy, who owns a farm—which of course explains the gun—and his son Leon, have always run all their power from a generator. This cut out in the early days of the Lockdown, which meant they didn't have any electricity to keep up to date with the news. Fortunately, they were always very self-sufficient, so they had plenty of food to survive on. Unfortunately, that meant by the time they were forced out of their home, they had long missed the meeting at the airport.

I can sense from the sadness in his eyes and the way his body language is almost retreating, that he lost someone during that time, but he doesn't divulge any information about this, so I don't push it. I bet it was Leon's mother, Randy's wife. I don't want to bring down the mood of the evening by getting someone to discuss their losses, so I allow him to tell his story in his own way.

The other family consists of Sarah and her two children, Ben and Emily. On closer inspection, I think Emily is about the same age as me, which puts me in a better mood. At least I'll have one friend here. They lived in the cottage next to the church—they're the vicar's family and he was a very strict, deeply religious man. He forced them to stay behind when everyone else left by plane—which means my suspicions were correct, and there isn't a refugee camp anywhere nearby. He insisted that they would be safe in the church, and that God's wrath needed to be faced, not fought.

"We noticed that he was infected a little while after we heard the planes leaving. It sent him madder as time progressed. We hid, frightened as he preached to us over and over that he had to '*leave the church and join his fellow comrades.*' He kept ranting that it was '*his mission from the Lord.*' It was awful. He fought his way out and we haven't seen him since."

I'm stunned into silence by Sarah's story. That's crazy. I'm actually kind of glad the vicar isn't here; I don't know how I would have tolerated the insane preacher with his scary God-fearing stories.

I wonder if he's one of the zombies hammering on the door.

"So we just…stayed. We didn't know what else to do. Everyone else had gone and we were terrified. I wouldn't have known how to begin looking after my children out there, with all of that danger." I'm starting to form a picture of their strict uptight lives as Sarah talks. I try to imagine Emily's teenage years—I bet she's the complete opposite to me. I barely had any restrictions growing up; my parents pretty much left me to my own devices. I guess they trusted me not to go off the rails and I never really did. The sad thing is, now I'll never get to. I'll always be alone so any rebellion will only hurt me. "I was just starting to get really panicky, wondering how we'd ever survive this, when Randy and Leon crashed in here. A bit like you did, I suppose." She smiles gratefully in his direction, and I notice a slight blush form on his cheeks.

Finally, the question I've been dying to answer is asked. "So did you want to stay here with us for a while?"

A smile plays on my lips as I answer, relief and happiness bursts from my chest. "Thank you so much, I'd love to. I'll do anything I can to help you out—" Sarah puts her hand up to stop me before I go off on a tangent, and indicates towards a sleeping bag, which I grab gratefully. The fatigue sets in again, I almost forgot how tired I was in all the excitement.

As I lie down I realise what all of this really means. I finally have another secure place to stay, with thick stone walls keeping the zombies away. Plus I have a group which, despite first impressions, are actually really friendly. You never know, they could turn out to be kind of awesome. Plus, we have a gun in our ranks, which can in no way be a bad thing.

Finally, after days of forcing my eyes open, I fall into a deep slumber.

CHAPTER 28

DR. JONES

March 13th

2:00 p.m.

I can't get my head around the newest orders from the higher ups. It's worse than anything I've ever been asked to do, ever. It's bordering on immoral. Do they expect me to have no heart just because I work in science? I know that's the stereotype, but people don't really believe that, do they? I'm sure there may be others who wouldn't think twice about doing something like this, considering it's for the greater good, but not me. My conscience shouts far too loudly.

It's fucked up, that's what it is. I can't

take much more of this. Are the people in charge psychopaths? No, maybe not. Maybe they do just want answers but this is just one step too far. Specimen 13.

13. James Max, 8

4"1', 49kg, dark brown eyes, dark brown hair.

No existing medical conditions.

Mother and three brothers still in camp.

At the moment he's in stage two. I've run all the standard tests on him. I'm just waiting for him to transgress into stage three. Then they want me to dissect him.

Yep, that's correct. You read it right! I have to dissect this child who isn't much older than Melody. I'm sat here, watching him die. Not a dignified death either, a horrifying, painful death. It's not right for this to happen to a child. It sad enough without knowing what's to come later. Once he's dead I have to contact the board, who will send in a soldier to put a bullet in his brain. That's when I have to do it.

I asked, I begged for it to be another

specimen. I'd still hate it, but the fact that it's a young child makes it a thousand times worse. Of course they know this. They refused my request. I know why—I've figured it all out, it's so obvious. They want to break me, to punish me for taking so long with this research. They think I should have fixed everything by now. So, they want to strip me of my humanity, make sure I'm more willing to do whatever they ask of me. They want to destroy any part of me that I have control over.

Nothing is sacred here. The people in charge are willing to go to extreme lengths to get their way. I can't even begin to imagine what the civilians are going through. It doesn't bear thinking about. If I'm suffering, they probably are too. I want to see Melody and Ashley, my need is getting more desperate by the day. If I do this, if I can just get through this task, complete their little 'test,' I'm going to demand that I visit them. If I really am the best that they have available, surely that gives me some *leverage? I've got to use that to my advantage. This needs to be more of a two-way street. I can't do all the giving.*

I've just got to do the unthinkable first.

6:15 p.m.

It's done. He's dead. I did exactly as I was told, ignoring the sensation that this whole thing was wrong. As I contacted the board, I thought about Ashley's face. When the soldier came in, armed and ready to shoot, I thought of Melody's face. I tried to ignore the blast and the blood. I tried to think about seeing my family again, but that horror will haunt my nightmares for a long time to come. The board have succeeded in damaging me in that way, at least.

Now his cadaver is laid on the workspace in front of me, taunting me. I can barely remember the moaning, violent beast he'd become, all I can see is the scared little boy calling out for his mummy as another wave of agony hit him. I have the scalpel in my hand, but I can't bring myself to act. Not yet.

If I put on my professional mind, and think about this act logically, it's the best thing to do. It really is the next step in my research, it could show up something that I've missed. But it's such a small body. It's a little boy that didn't deserve this. His life was cut far too short. Now he is being spared the right to a humane death, his family won't be able to hold a funeral for him. I doubt they'll even be told what's become of him. I wish I could tell them, I wish I could ease my conscience by letting them know that it wasn't all my fault. But they'd probably rip me to shreds for my part in all of this.

8:45 p.m.

Results from the autopsy:

After performing the typical Y shape incision from the shoulders to the sternum, and opening the chest cavity, the organs were exposed.

They were almost entirely black,

shrivelled, as if they had not been in use for years, never mind hours. I removed all the organs one by one, using the en masse technique of Letulle. They could have almost fallen apart in my hands. This merely confirmed what I'd already seen in the MRI scans.

Then I opened up the heart. An outpour of gangrenous pus spilled out. And the same for the lungs, the kidneys, the liver. I'll read up on this, research further into this as I have a feeling it's somehow key.

1:10 a.m.

I keep reading over the data from the autopsy, wondering where to go from here. I need another brain. I need someone else to come in on this and help me. I've hit a brick wall in my research. Maybe pride has stopped me demanding assistance so far, but no more. I want to find an answer to this, I want to go back to my normal life, I do really want to help everyone that has survived and I can no longer do it alone.

Sometimes even discussing findings with others leads to answers. Just running over ideas and debating opinions. I'm sure many revelations have been stumbled across in this way.

Tomorrow things are going to change around here.

**NB: Specimens one, four, five, and seven were removed from my laboratory today.*

CHAPTER 29

ALYSSA

I awaken as the coloured rays of light stream through the window. My night was filled with bizarre and vivid dreams. I always get like that when I'm really tired and have a deep night's sleep. At first I was confused to find myself surrounded by pews, it took a while for my brain to connect, for the memories to come flooding back.

As the previous day's events crash into my mind, happiness fills my entire being. I did it. I set myself a goal and I pulled out all the stops to achieve it. I'm actually here, inside the church that I've been staring at for days from the top of the hill that now feels a million miles away.

Suddenly, I'm aware of noise surrounding me, coming from every direction. Everyone else is up and busy doing jobs around the building. I blush at my laziness, immediately worrying about what everyone must think of me. I pull myself up quickly and rush over to Sarah, who is hand washing clothes.

"Sorry, sorry. I didn't mean…what can I do to help?"

"Don't be silly." She brushes me off. "I don't need help, but you certainly needed that sleep. Just rest today, you've obviously been though a lot."

"I don't want you to think—"

"I don't think anything, none of us do. Now go on, let me get on." She smiles reassuringly and there's nothing I can do but nod. I don't want to be seen as the person that doesn't pull her weight. I'll just have to make up for it tomorrow.

As I look around at everyone else, I notice Randy is missing. I question Sarah about this.

"He's out gathering supplies." I can hear the strain in her voice as she says this. She's clearly worried about losing someone else. I wonder if there's anything deeper in her feelings, but instantly dismiss the idea. They've both recently lost loved ones; they've learnt the hard way not to care too deeply for anyone in the apocalypse. Feelings get you killed. "Maybe he'll even find some other survivors while he's out there. I think you've given us all a glimmer of hope." She laughs, but the sound is hollow.

I start wondering if he'll find E on his travels. If he's looking it's totally possible. I try to picture what the mysterious person will look like, but I don't have a single thing to go on, even the gender. I can feel a longing in the pit of my stomach starting to develop. A need to find E…to meet the person who has written all of these notes. Without them, I might not have made it this far. I might have given up long ago. Maybe I'll offer to go out with Randy next time. He's bound to say yes, I've already proved my worth as a fighter, and then I can assist in the search. The sooner the mystery is solved, the better. Not just for my peace of mind, but because knowing someone else is out there, alone and unprotected, isn't a pleasant thought.

For now, I need to find a way to amuse myself. All this relaxing is giving me too much time to think. I'll start getting restless if I stay like this, and I really *want* to like it here, I want to be satisfied with this group of people, even if they aren't what I initially expected. I look around at the others. The two young boys are playing with some toy cars they must have found at some point. I can't help thinking that it's nice they have each other; I don't know how they'd cope with the boredom alone. If I struggled in the B and B, I dread to think how hard it would be for a child who wouldn't fully understand the severity of the situation.

They look around the same age as Lexi. I try to picture her playing alongside them. I bet she would've loved it here. She may have struggled with everything up until this point, but I think having kids her own age would've been great for her. As I try to remember my little sister, I realise I'm already struggling to recall all of her features. It's like my memory of her is already blurry, affected by the way she died. The zombie virus has wiped out all my happy thoughts of Lexi. I didn't even pick up any photographs of my family when I left. I was so focused on essentials and not getting sentimental, that I didn't even grab anything to remember them by.

I drag my attention away to Emily before I get too upset. She's in the corner reading, really concentrating on the book in front of her. She was cleaning earlier, but I guess this is what she does when she finishes her daily chores. It's not as if there is a lot else to do for anyone our age. Too old to play, but too young to fully contribute. I wonder if she'll be glad of my presence, if having someone her own age here will be a blessing for her. I know it is for me, but I can't quite work her out yet. She seems quiet, and maybe a little unsociable—she certainly hasn't made any effort with me yet.

Then again, maybe that's a downside of being a preacher's daughter. She's obviously been brought up *very* differently than me, so we may not get on at all. We could be far too different to be friends. I really hope that isn't the case. She's the closest thing I've got to decent, fun company. I know survival is top priority in the zombie apocalypse, but I've spent too much time being nothing but miserable. I've realised how important amusement really is. I decide not to disturb her while her head is in her book, in case that sparks an instant dislike of me. It's been so long since I've been around people my age I don't even know how to act anymore, it's weird.

I sit down on one of the hard wooden pews and let out a big sigh. Again I find a disappointed feeling settling over me. This just *isn't* going as planned. I might have a nice group, but they aren't the fantasy I'd built up in my head. That's the downside to being a dreamer; real life can never match up to your expectations. I wanted fun, excitement, adventure. Not cleaning, chores, and tedium. I think I'm more suited to the dangerous, outside tasks. However much I struggle with them at the time, the feeling of accomplishment after it's over makes it all worth it.

I must have huffed louder than I intended to, because I suddenly notice that Emily is staring at me with a bemused expression on her face. I mouth "*sorry*" and a smile flickers across her lips in response. I catch a glimpse of something, a personality that I didn't notice before, maybe a cheeky side? I think I might have disregarded her too quickly. Maybe there's a lot more to this girl than meets the eye. I shuffle over as I see her lower and close her book. I intend to grab this opportunity with both hands and break the ice. If I can get a communication flowing, maybe things will pick up for me. I don't want to be ungrateful and unsatisfied with what I have. I have to make the best of this situation—it's the best one I've had since the Lockdown began.

"Hi, Emily…right?"

"Yeah, and you're Alyssa?" And this is all it takes for us to begin talking—I don't know what I was so afraid of!

It doesn't take me long to realise that Emily is just shy and reserved, but once you get her talking she's actually really funny. As time wears on, I feel happier and much more positive and we chat and laugh. Soon, we stumble across the topic that is clearly her forte—science. As soon as I mentioned the virus, her eyes lit up and she became overly animated. It turns out she has a whole notebook of theories that she's been working on, which she pulls out to show me.

Wow.

And I thought my knowledge was extensive. Emily knows a million percent more than me about AM13—it's crazy. This girl is super smart. I've never met anyone quite like her, I'm in awe. As she starts to lose me with jargon that I don't understand, I find myself staring at her lips, rather than concentrating on her words. They're plump and dark pink, and her bright white teeth shine through the gap as she smiles, which she does a lot when she's passionate about what she's saying. When she catches me looking, I force my eyes to snap away quickly, blushing heavily, the heat reaching my ears.

That's weird; I don't know what's wrong with me.

After that awkward moment, I find it hard to look her directly in the eye. I wonder if my acute embarrassment is obvious. If it is, it hasn't stopped her in her tracks, because she quickly shows me diagrams, reports, graphs, and all sorts of other research that she's compiled—she could write a book with all that she has! She's actually been spending the zombie apocalypse doing homework. Who does that? It's insane, even in my own boredom I would *never* have gone this far. She should be working for the government, trying to stop all of this.

Of course, she could've been if she'd gotten on the plane. If her father hadn't forced her to wait here to die. Her brains could have been used for the greater good.

Randy returns later that afternoon, alone but with a good stock of food, so a good dinner is ahead of us. We sit and eat together again, which is such a novelty for me. Even before all of this, my family used to eat separately because we were all always so busy with our different schedules. It's really nice eating, talking, and laughing. It certainly beats all the lonely nights at the B and B. I feel like I have a little family around me, and I'm enjoying the company of everyone. Why didn't I do this sooner? I'm so glad I'm here.

Later that evening, I pull Randy to one side to speak to him privately. There's still a little issue that's concerning me. It isn't anything major, but I need to clear it up before it becomes a big problem in my head. "Why were you confused yesterday when I was talking about the zombies?" I ask him.

"We just never thought of the infected in that way." His answer poses many more questions, but I don't ask them. I need to accept that not everyone views the world the same way that I do. I've got to be more understanding of others' opinions, especially now that I'm a part of a group.

CHAPTER 30

DR. JONES

March 14th

9:30 a.m.

I've had my meeting. This morning. Suffice to say that it didn't go well. The board members somehow managed to talk me around into not seeing my family for now. As I sit here, in my little office, alone, I've got no idea how. I had everything planned out. I knew exactly what I was going to say, but somehow they twisted and manipulated my words and by the end of it, I felt guilty for even asking. I felt bad for requesting to see my own wife and child.

Sneaky, manipulative bastards. Is that

how politics works these days?

I remember feeling awful as I then had to stammer out the words about needing some assistance for this work. What did they do to me to make me feel this way? How did I feel ashamed for needing help? This isn't your average project. I'm so angry at them, but more at myself. One of them said that they've 'noted my request' and they will 'look into it for me—hopefully find a virologist or a researcher.' Why don't I believe them? I've come out of that meeting more convinced than ever that the rest of my time will be spent in this laboratory alone. I'm going to have to figure this whole mess out by myself. I don't feel confident about that!

I'm getting two new specimens this afternoon. The ones I currently have are no longer useful. They've all been in stage three for a while now, and are way past any humanity, and I haven't even glanced their way for a few days. I'm only interested in specimens that I can obtain information from.

It's not that I don't care anymore. I still feel so much sympathy for them, but my desperation to find some sort of answer is starting to override anything else.

I get the impression that the board is going to continue passing all the camp members that display any signs of infection on to me, unsure of what else they can do with them. Honestly, I can't see any new tests that I can run at this stage. All I'm really doing is ruling possibilities out. As useful as that is, I want a more positive response.

No, what I really want is to see Ashley and Melody, even for 30 seconds. I just want to hold my wife's face in my hands, I just want to hug my daughter. Why is that so much to ask? Is it some sort of motivational tactic? Or just more punishment? I can't bear much more. I think I'm going a little stir crazy—I can't decide if I'm very paranoid, or if my suspicions are correct. If the board members truly are evil, it doesn't *bode well for any of our futures.*

11:45 a.m.

14. Rachael Lawrence, 25, Office Manager.

5"8, 58kg, brown eyes, long dark red hair.

No existing medical conditions.

Her husband and baby are still in camp.

She was brought in during stage two, but had progressed to the final stage before the soldiers had even left. I've never seen a transformation happen so quickly. She is vicious, violent, and highly enraged. Could this be personality related? Or is it just random, like every other effect seems to be? Unfortunately, without knowing her beforehand, I can't theorise this.

15. Jason White, 32, English Professor.

6"0', 62kg, green eyes, blond hair.

Existing medical condition—Renal Cell Carcinoma.

He's still in stage one. Showing minimal symptoms at the current time.

Jason White. What to say about Jason. He's...different; I don't know how to describe him in this document. If it wasn't for the very large bite mark on his forearm, I would be hard pushed to believe he's infected at all. I do wonder how he managed to get bitten inside the camp but I haven't dared ask him. I feel uncomfortable around the specimens now considering the negative reception I've received up until this point. I'm a hated figure—which makes a whole lot of sense even if it isn't fairly deserved.

He's very coherent and has actually been very friendly to me. I just haven't brought my own walls down yet. It's very difficult not to immediately like him though, which is dangerous territory. I have to keep reminding myself not to get attached. Soon he will die, just like the others. If I let myself like him, even a little bit, I'm sure the board will find some way to use that against me. I need to keep detached, because of what they could make me do to him. I can't go through another incident like the dissection. I still haven't recovered from that.

As he speaks to me, I have to keep repeating to myself 'he's going to die, he's going to die.' It's terribly morbid, but I need to separate myself from them. I have to.

1:40 p.m.

I've already broken my promise. I've already engaged in a very long conversation with Jason. Despite everything I said previously, I have spent the last couple of hours thoroughly enjoying his company. I couldn't help myself, it's been far too long since I had someone who wasn't in the painful throes of infection to talk to. I'm weak I know, but I'm sure anyone would succumb in my circumstances. Wouldn't they?

It all started when I was taking a blood sample. I couldn't stop my eyes from fixating on the terribly gory wound on his arm. He noticed, of course. I wasn't being discreet, but with all the other specimens I haven't had to be. Instead of calling me out on my *imprudence, he asked me about all of my research in an extremely calm tone of voice. I nervously started to tell him a little, because I didn't want to completely ignore his queries, but I had to say it without giving away too many details. How do you tell someone that the illness they have is a certain death sentence?*

It turns out I didn't need to worry. He's already aware of the terrible details. He already knew that AM13 has 100% mortality rate, but he didn't seem too bothered. In fact, his manner didn't waver from upbeat.

Of course, he's very familiar with low survival rates. He was diagnosed with a very aggressive form of kidney cancer a few years ago and has been living on borrowed time for a while. I was amazed with his positive attitude as he told me all of this. He hasn't let any of it get him down at all. In fact, he's been living a good quality of life focusing on minute to minute.

I can't help thinking that I could learn a

lot from Jason.

I've spent my time in this confinement miserable and lonely. I've been allowing my emotions to get tangled up in a web of rage and confusion. I've spent far too much time worrying about things that I've got no control over. What I should've been doing is focusing on my opportunity to have a positive impact on the planet. I need to stop concocting conspiracy theories about the board members in my mind, for all I know they could just be as desperate as I am for me to find an answer. And that's what I need to do.

7:50 p.m.

I've now spent the rest of the evening talking and laughing with Jason. I haven't sent him back to his enclosure and I don't intend to. I can't degrade this man, especially when he poses no real threat to me. I'm just going to leave it unlocked for the time being so he can come and go as he pleases. He just feels more like a friend to me *than a specimen and even though it probably isn't my wisest decision, I feel more comfortable with it than any of the other choices I've made whilst in this room. Sure, there'll come a time when this will have to change, but living minute to minute, this is the best thing for both of us.*

In fact, Jason took it upon himself to start routing through the cupboards, to find some entertainment. He actually managed to dig out a dusty old chess set, which appears to have been abandoned for many years. Of course, this led to a challenge and my competitive streak just couldn't say no. To my utter embarrassment, he absolutely annihilated me. He's amazing! I always thought I was a great chess player, it takes a certain kind of intellect and patience, and I thought I had it nailed. Jason made me view myself in a whole new light.

During this game, I told him with more confidence about everything I've achieved so far. Although he hasn't got any scientific knowledge, he does have the fresh perspective that I've been craving. I'm finding talking about my research very therapeutic. He's given me a well needed boost of enthusiasm. He's made me feel like I can achieve this, that I need to do it. In fact, I'm even rethinking my opinion on creating a cure. If I can do it, if I can save even a few people like Jason who don't have extensive bodily damage, I should do it, shouldn't I? It's my moral responsibility. It's got to be the right thing to do.

10:35 p.m.

The results from Jason's tests show something very surprising. Something I didn't expect. His cancer treatment drugs seem to have a bizarre 'slowing down effect' on the virus. I'm going to ensure that he keeps up with his medication just so I can confirm this theory. At this point, anything is still possible. It's an interesting concept, at any rate. At least it's shown me something new—I haven't had that for a long while.

The results from specimen fourteen's tests

don't show me anything noteworthy, unfortunately. There's no obvious reason why her body has reacted so aggressively to AM13. Just another random occurrence, I assume. This virus is full of them, which makes this research all the more challenging.

CHAPTER 31

ALYSSA

Three days later, I overhear Randy discussing another supply run with Sarah. A fission of excitement bubbles away in my stomach as I think about the prospect of going with him. I've been feeling a little bit of cabin fever stuck inside these walls. It's been growing since I first arrived and I've hated the slight discomfort with myself. This is the obvious way to cure this, as a way to find satisfaction in my new environment. It's the best I could have hoped for, and I *do* love it here, I really like all of the people, especially Emily. We've started to develop a fantastic friendship, despite our palpable differences.

I wait impatiently for them to finish their conversation before bounding over and proposing the idea to Randy. A wary look fills his eyes as I speak and I can tell he thinks I'll be a liability. I try to convince him, I use everything I've got, all my persuasive tactics, and eventually I start to wear him down. After all, it wasn't a coincidence that I lasted so long alone, is it? He knows I can fight, he knows I'm smart. When we get out there, and I *know* I'll be going, I'll prove myself worthy.

The next morning, I get a very begrudging "*yes*" and I'm over the moon. I knew he'd crack of course, I knew he wouldn't be able to resist my offer. Before we leave, he makes a quick trip over to Sarah's cottage. It isn't far from the church, so it's a fairly safe journey, but the house is very exposed so no one goes there without a good purpose. He's gone to pick up a selection of new clothes, to give Sarah a bit of a break from washing. I think he's getting worried about her; she does seem to be becoming more disconnected from us all as the days pass by. I barely know her, of course, so I can't have too strong an opinion, but I know Emily has concerns.

When he returns with a large mishmash of items in his hands, we all root through them excitedly. Although these clothes belong to Sarah, Emily, Ben, and the vicar, none of them mind us helping ourselves. I pick my clothes carefully, wanting to look good for my mission. When I can sense a big event such as this arriving, the film set floods my mind again. I find dark denim skinny jeans, which are only slightly too big, a long sleeve black t-shirt and combat boots. I'm so glad they're in my size. I look down at myself, wishing I had a mirror, and thinking this outfit suits my upcoming role well. It isn't too different from my 'uniform' pre-zombies, so on top of looking great, it's comfortable too. Of course, my hair is matted and unwashed, but you can't have everything. If I tightly pin it back, you can hardly tell how gross it is. I sling an empty backpack over my shoulder, ready to be filled with whatever spoils we manage to collect today and I grab my muddy, blood-covered axe. I'm ready to go.

I'm actually really excited about this mission. I haven't had to scavenge for anything yet, I had things really easy at the B and B, so I'm eager for the new adventure. A part of me is frightened too, of course, but I push those feelings to one side, determined to feel only the positive emotions. I imagine myself telling this story to future generations, maybe even my own children. I imagine their eyes lighting up with awe as I talk about my bravery, about my unselfish decision to go out and gather supplies for my fellow group members.

I say a quick goodbye to everyone, not wanting to make a big deal out of leaving. That will just allow the nerves to kick in. A sad smile plays on Emily's lips as she mouths a quiet goodbye my way. I can see that she's worried about losing me, her first decent friend since the apocalypse began. I try to convey to her that I'll be fine with my eyes, but I'm not sure it comes across well.

My heart is racing with anticipation as the doors creak open, and a slither of light sneaks through the crack, blinding us for a second. We can't quite see around to the door via the window, so we have no idea how many zombies we are going to be immediately faced with. I'm ready for it though, I'm prepared.

"Argh!" I scream as I slice my axe through a disgusting, pus bag's head. Luckily there were only four zombies outside, which was no problem for me and Randy. I shoot him a quick smile as I take out another with ease, and I think I see a bit of awe in his expression. I'm pleased that I've managed to impress so early on. I can't help but hope that the others are watching me at this moment too. Well, Emily mostly. She's so smart; I want her to see that I have worth too.

As soon as the nearby zombies have been taken care of, we take off quickly, wanting to get back before the church gets overly surrounded again. I follow behind Randy, unsure of where we're heading. Despite all of my time running through the town, I still don't know it very well. I was so focused on the church, I didn't notice much else.

We end up at a large shopping centre. We're both panting as Randy tells me his plan. "This is the nearest half-decent place to the church. Obviously we want to get back before it gets dark so I didn't want to go too far. If you want, get some medical supplies—you know, antibiotics, bandages, that sort of thing. You never know when we might need any of that stuff and I'd much rather have it already with us. I'll get some more food. While we're out, I might as well stock up a bit more. We'll meet back at the entrance ASAP."

I gulp, trying not to make a big deal out of the fact that we'll be splitting up. I wasn't really prepared for that. I *did* insist on tagging along, and I am used to being alone. I just need to do this. Get through it and I'll have full respect. I've just…never gone into the lion's den willingly before. I may be brave, but I'm not stupid. Stupidity gets you killed. Emotions rise through my throat like bile so I clamp my mouth shut and nod curtly. I don't want Randy to even see a flicker of fear or negativity cross my features for even a split second. I'm not a kid; I really need him to see that I'm just as capable as he is.

We move in slowly. Everything seems quiet. I start to wonder if someone has already been in here and cleaned the place out. I open my mouth to ask Randy if this is somewhere that he's visited before, when a crashing sound comes from nowhere. I emit a small squeal before I can stop myself, and immediately try to cover it up with a cough. Randy isn't paying any attention to me, he's on high alert. His gun is held high, aiming in a variety of locations, trying to focus in on its target. How is he so calm?

Nothing happens. Not at first. Randy signals at me to keep moving, so I keep close to him. My heartbeat thunders, my eyes tingle with water. I hate this anticipation, I wish whatever is going to happen would just get on with it. It's the waiting that I can't stand. I can hear all sorts of small sounds in every direction. I'm not sure which of them are real and which have been created by my overactive imagination.

A growl, right behind me. This one I know for sure is genuine I spin round; ready to defend myself but before I can even move Randy has plunged a knife into its forehead, forcing blood and filth to cover me. I watch in amazement as it slumps to the ground, its life rapidly ebbing away. He did that so quickly I didn't even notice it happening. He's already moving on, not even reacting to what just happened. Is he just so used to things like that? Do they no longer scare him? And if he didn't see them as zombies, how did he know to kill them like that? I try to think back to the news reports, maybe they instructed this sort of thing, but it's so hard to distinguish what I heard, what I read, and what I already knew about zombies.

"Okay, so as we discussed, we'll meet back here as soon as we've got everything. If I'm any longer than 20 minutes or anything happens to make you feel insecure, head back to the church—you know the way—and I won't be far behind you. Don't, under *any* circumstances, allow yourself to get hurt."

He turns on his heel and is gone before I can reply, before I can tell him that I don't actually remember the way, I was too focused on following his footsteps to notice landmarks on the journey. I shake my head and take a deep breath, promising myself that there's no point in worrying, it won't even come to that. I look around, realising I don't even know where to begin in this place. I've never been here to know the location of any of the shops.

I force my feet to move. I'm sure it won't be too difficult to locate what I'm looking for, and standing still certainly isn't going to get me anywhere. My heart beat is screaming loudly, my brain buzzing with thoughts, making it very hard to hear anything else. Movement. I heard something, I'm sure I did. My eyes flicker around in every direction; my body is ready to fight. My pulse rate increases rapidly, my head starts to ache with tension.

Nothing. It's nothing. I've got to stop it. The zombie Randy killed has got me paranoid. I don't know why I'm feeling so frightened, I've been through a lot worse. Get a grip, Alyssa.

I continue to creep until eventually I turn a corner and find myself face to face with a pharmacy. The relief of this sight calms me right down. Any more fear might have given me a heart attack. I quickly sprint in, eager for this mission to be over. Much as I'm glad to be outside, being useful, I can't wait to return and know I'm safe. Then I can reflect on all of this and see the positive aspects with hindsight. I grab boxes of all kinds of medication; pain killers, insulin, antibiotics, a first aid box, anything I can get my hands on. This is a really good idea. Any illness in the zombie apocalypse can be the death of you. It isn't exactly like medical care is easily accessible. It's a huge possibility which people probably don't consider until it's too late. I feel a little smug at how prepared my group is.

My brain concocts another noise which makes me violently jump, only this time when I spin around, my face smacks straight into a man's chest. It was real this time, I wasn't just paranoid. After a split second of panic, I raise my axe, trying to get it above my head, only to feel it come lose and be pulled out of my grip. I try to grasp tighter, but my palms have become silky and useless with sweat.

"Hey, hey," a calm voice immediately eradicates

the possibility of zombies. "There's no need for that, little lady."

I look up to find out where the smooth voice is coming from, just to find myself faced with an extremely handsome man, who's probably in his early 20's. I'm stunned into silence—his crinkly, infectious smile wiping any possible witty remark right out of my mouth. He's very tall, about six feet, with pale red hair and sparkly blue eyes. He has a cool preppy look about him—underneath all the dirt and grime. I can just imagine how many girls have fallen at his feet, unable to resist him. In the old life anyway.

"Erm, I, uh—" I stutter, unable to form words. I can't get my brain to engage, I can't make it power my voice box. What's happening to me? I've never found myself rendered quite so speechless. I can see he's amused as my face gets hotter. I hate looking like an idiot and it's making me even more flustered.

Finally he breaks the silence, trying to put my obvious discomfort at ease. "May I ask what you're doing here?" I find him so incredibly likable that I start to unwind just from those few words. I don't even *consider* distrusting him.

Conscious of time, I tell him a very short, abridged version of the events that led me to here. "Long story short, a group of us are staying in a church nearby. We've just come out on a supply run, I'm not actually by myself, but I've got to get back soon, so if I could please get my axe back, that'd be great." I keep looking over my shoulder, trying to highlight the fact that I really need to go. I desperately hope that he doesn't ask me for more details. Now just isn't the time to go into my whole saga.

He doesn't answer immediately so I attempt a different tact. I try pleading with him through my eyes. I try to get across that I can't leave without my weapon. I feel naked and exposed without it. I start to feel frustration bubbling up inside me. I don't need this right now. Isn't the fact that it's the zombie apocalypse bad enough?

Eventually he laughs, showing me that he was messing with me. I don't appreciate that at all. I glare at him under my eyelashes, not wanting to escalate the situation, but wanting him to know that I'm annoyed.

Then his expression turns serious. "Okay, I'll make a deal with you. I'm sick of being here by myself. If I can come back with you, join you at the church, you can have your axe back."

Initially I'm stumped. Of course I understand his dilemma—I was in the same position myself not so long ago. I know that it's much safer being with others. Plus, who knows what skills he could possess. He does look very strong and able. I try to picture him fitting in with the group. They *were* very accepting of me, and Randy did say he wanted to find others. In fact, the more I think it over, the more the obvious answer has to be yes.

I nod silently, unable to trust myself to speak. I'm really hoping Randy is okay with my decision, even though it's never been appointed; he's clearly the leader of us all. I can't think of any reason why he wouldn't be, but I feel really cheeky making the decision for the group.

As we walk, a thought hits me. "Are you by any chance E?" I hold my breath, praying for him to say he is. I think everyone will be glad to find the mystery person who has been leaving us all messages. That'll make my decision seem more rational.

Unfortunately he shakes his head. "I've seen a message from someone calling themselves E though around town. I'm actually called Pete. How about you?"

"Alyssa," I answer flatly, disappointed. I can't believe after all this time I still don't know who left that note for me in the airport. Now that I know E is still alive, I wish they'd just reveal themselves. Whoever it is must have seen some sign that we're all still here. So many of us have seen the messages, E must have seen at least one of us.

Luckily Randy is at the entrance of the shopping centre waiting for me. He's immediately on the defensive as he spots the man behind me. It does look as if I'm being held hostage, or being threatened. Pete is looming over me, gripping onto my axe, while I dejectedly shuffle in front of him.

I hold my hands up. "Don't worry, Randy; it's not as bad as it looks." He doesn't relax his stance. "Pete just wants to come back with us, if that's okay with you? He's been here by himself for some time."

"I'll have to see what everyone else thinks," he states, buying himself some time. "Why don't you tell us about yourself while we walk back? Let me get to know you a bit." Randy's being smart with this one—learning all he can about Pete before making a decision.

"Sure, thanks." Pete smiles widely before launching into his own zombie apocalypse story. "I never trusted the government, even before all of this kicked off. They're just so corrupt, you know?" I nod, even though I don't have any idea what he's talking about. "Well, I knew the Lockdown was never going to work, the AM13 virus was absolutely raging out of control before they even attempted to get a handle of it. I stayed in, of course, I'd have been absolutely crazy not to, but I knew it wouldn't be long until they had to do something else.

When the news came that they wanted us to fly off to some exotic, supposed safe haven I knew I wasn't going to go along. The government have no idea what to do and I wasn't going to get myself killed for another ridiculous plan of theirs—I bet no one survived *that* journey. So I stayed here, living day by day, minute by minute. I've been moving around a lot. That's how I survive. I don't think staying in one place for longer than 24 hours is a good idea, that way I never risk getting myself surrounded. I've still been through a lot of terrible things, I'm sure we all have to have survived this far, but I do my best to prevent killing where I can."

I listen intently to his words, trying to picture his experience. It sounds so wildly different to mine, but not in a good way. Personally I think the constant moving sounds exhausting. That idea seems even worse than me stuck bored and alone!

CHAPTER 32

DR. JONES

March 17th

12:20 p.m.

I don't know what I can write here anymore. I have no further progress to report. It's all the same. The specimens come through in various stages. They go through stage one and two and end up in stage three. No matter what, that's what happens. The process might be slightly different and happen at different rates for each specimen, but the end result is the same. I really don't think there is anything anyone can do to stop it.

No matter what tests I run, what

research I do, or even what angle I look at it from, there is no rhyme or reason for why it affects people differently. I think I could look forever more and not find anything out. It's just 'one of those things.' This virus is full of anomalies.

I don't know what to do now. I've been feeling more and more desolate as the days go by. The board is breathing down my neck, demanding results, and I don't know what I can say to them. If I tell them that I've come to the end of everything I can do, they'll kill me. I just know it. I don't want to die without at least seeing Ashley and Melody. I can't allow that to happen. I need them; they deserve to hear all that I've done wrong. They need my apology and I want to give it.

As the days whizz past, I've been spending more and more time playing chess with Jason. He is still unbeaten, it's amazing. I know this is a huge waste of time, but it's utterly miserable watching people change from humans to former shells of themselves.

Everyone that comes through here is going to end up going through a painful, terrifying death. I don't know how much more of it I can stand. It's utterly demoralising. Without blowing off some steam, I think my mind would collapse under the mental strain. I never planned to allow myself so much pressure in my career. I was always happy in my role, I haven't ever been one of the overly ambitious, determined to get to the top. I only took this job to ease my guilt and because I was so sure I'd be more of an assistant. I never suspected I'd be the leading scientist. I wouldn't have even considered taking the job if I had.

The chess games are the only thing that's keeping me going. It's uplifting to have something else to focus on that takes my entire attention. It's escapism. The conversation with Jason is rarely about AM13 anymore. I'll occasionally discuss theories with him, but I much prefer learning about his life before this disease came along to control it, and it's a weight *off my shoulders to discuss mine. Pre-virus tales remind me that there's much more to life than the board members and this little room. Without Jason, without chess, I wouldn't be able to function.*

Even my dreams are filled with bites and blood and death. I wake up so many times during the night—heart pounding, covered in sweat—and the nightmare doesn't end there. I can't break away from it. It's so difficult to return to sleep with the growling and screaming infiltrating my mind. The nightmare continues, whatever I do.

I don't know how much longer I can fend the insanity off. When Jason goes, the madness will consume me quickly, I'm sure. I don't want to think about the prospect of him ending up as dead as the others because I can't bear it. In the dark of the night, when the tears start to roll down my cheeks, I can't focus on anything else.

Luckily for now, he hasn't progressed anywhere near into stage two. In fact, all of his flu-like symptoms seem to have vanished.

He still has traces of AM13 in his blood stream, of course, a clear sign that he's still dying. Although the cancer drugs still seem to be slowing it down, they aren't powerful enough to stop it.

Jason's cancer treatments include:

Monoclonal Antibodies—Panitumumab, 'target therapy,' targets and attacks cancerous cells.

Immunotherapy—Bevacizumab, encourages immune system to attack cancerous cells.

Angiogenesis Inhibitor Therapy—Intraconazole, inhibits the growth of new blood vessels.

He has previously been involved with chemotherapy, radiotherapy, and hormonal treatments, but this is the current medication he's taking, and has been since the Lockdown.

The next stage for me is to separate these medications to figure out which one of these is having an effect on AM13. I can't do this within Jason, which would provide the most effective response, without endangering him, so I'll have to do it the old-fashion laboratory way—test tubes, etc.

At the moment, Jason's the only specimen I'm continuing to run tests on. The others are all in stage three, without any humanity at all, and at this point I don't see what else they can show me. I can't see any point in endangering lives just to learn what I already know. Jason is showing me new things. His medication holds some sort of answer; I just need to work out what this is.

It's the only lead I have at the moment so I have no other choice. I'm praying that this will help me find a way to create an antidote. I hope I'm right to pursue this path.

3:30 p.m.

I can't help but wonder who put these idiots in charge? Who decided that they were going to control this encampment? I certainly didn't vote for them. I can't imagine that they were part of the government beforehand; they seem to have a terribly brutal way of going about things. It feels more like a dictatorship. I can't help but be suspicious when the threats against me become more violent.

They never say anything outright, but to be honest, they don't have to. The meaning is very clear. This time it was subtle threats suggested that I'm never going to see my family again. That's inhumane—they won't be able to continue treating people this way when life eventually returns to normal, people won't stand for it. Right now, things are up in the air, confusing, hard to deal with, but soon they'll get their comeuppance.

I feel hollow. I should feel sad, angry, frustrated. But I don't. I just feel empty.

When I came here, I just accepted them as the leaders because they told me they were. Is that how they forced themselves in charge? Maybe no one thought to argue with them. I wonder if life for civilians is as bad as it is for me. I wonder if they are run in such a tight fisted manner. Or maybe they're *just left alone because they haven't got a job to do, a purpose to fulfil. I'm sure I'd have heard about rioting and rebellion if things were that bad, wouldn't I? I don't really know how cut off I am from everything. I just can't help but imagine these things happening.*

For me, things are reaching their boiling point. It isn't going to be long before things become really dire. I've got to get on; I need to make some kind of progress before the next time I see them. I don't want anything bad to happen to me or my family. I'm so scared for them. Much more than for myself.

I told Jason to stop distracting me with chess. I tried to pretend it was all in good humour with a weak smile and he responded by telling me I was just chicken. But we both know that things are going downhill. He knows how serious things are becoming, it's obvious. In fact in light of this, for the past hour, he's been acting as my assistant.

It's a sign of how awful this virus and the situation is when one of the specimens is helping the scientist that's experimenting on him.

I really hope we both make it out of here alive. We deserve to, we haven't done anything to deserve the harsh lifestyle that's been thrust upon us.

CHAPTER 33

ALYSSA

I can't believe how annoying Pete has become already. He's messing absolutely everything up. I almost wish we'd left him behind at the shopping centre. I wish Randy had dug his heels in and refused to bring him along. I know that thought is really cruel, but I'm just so frustrated. He keeps talking all the time about moving. He's trying to convince everyone that we need to constantly keep changing our location, in the way he has been doing up until now. I can't see the point of that. Why put ourselves in unnecessary risk when we have a good thing going right here?

The real issue is, as the days pass and the more he puts the idea into everyone's minds, the more zombies seem to be surrounding us. I don't know if they're finally wising up to our scent, or if our trips outside have led them back to where we are. I don't know where their intelligence levels are at. I have my own preconceived notions, but I can't rely solely on them.

During one of Pete's rants, I suggested that he up and go it alone and leave us be, but Sarah got really angry at me for that. She's far too kind-hearted to see him as he really is. She's the sort of person that likes to see the best in everyone. That's not a *bad* quality necessarily, but I do think it could put her in avoidable danger. The worst thing is Pete has a charm and charisma that I can see slowly winning everybody over, one by one. My mood is becoming more thunderous by the second. If they all decide to follow him, I don't know what I'll do.

Emily has been colder towards me since we returned. If I try to discuss my annoyance with her, she ends up snapping at me. "Well, it's your fault he's here in the first place." I don't know what has got her so rattled and she won't tell me. I've tried to talk to her, I've tried giving her space, and nothing seems to work. I'm finding this negative quality in her hard work on top of everything else. If I've done something to upset her, I'd rather she just tell me. I can't stand having to second guess myself all the time. I've got far too much else to worry about. To be honest, this struggle is all new to me. Emily is the first person whose opinion has mattered to me. No one else has been in my life long enough to have any impact.

If I try to discuss my issue with anyone else, the frustration just bubbles out of me and I end up coming across as irrational and hot-headed. I just can't seem to keep my cool. I can feel everyone slowly drifting away from me. It's as heart-wrenching as it is enraging. I thought I was starting to earn respect here, I thought my outlook mattered. Why is everyone so quick to listen to the newcomer? He hasn't been forced to earn his respect in the way I feel like I have.

* * *

Predictably, something soon happens to sway everyone's decision permanently. A zombie finally manages to crack the glass of one of the stained glass windows and the constant clawing is making the hole bigger. All the others become far too terrified too quickly and begin acting irrationally. I'm sure if we just secure the place better, we would be able to stay, but no one even pauses for a second for me to say any of this.

Of course, I can see their logic. This place was never going to last forever and while the zombie army grows outside, soon we won't be able to leave at all and we'll end up starving to death, but right now I'm far too fractious to allow myself to see any common sense.

Frustrated tears prick my eyes as I squeeze my fists in temper. I'm watching everyone gather up their belongings rapidly around me and I *want* to refuse to leave. I want to stand my ground and insist everyone listen to me but I know it's far too late for that. I'm not ready to say goodbye to this place yet. As unsatisfied as I've found myself feeling, it's the best 'home' I've had since the zombie apocalypse started.

I stalk off over to my things and hold my sleeping bag between my fingers. I sense another person approaching behind me. "Pete, if that's you trying to put your arms around me, I swear I'll—" I trail off as I turn to see a distinctly female face in front of me. Emily. At the sight of her, the tears start rolling. I can't even begin to stop them. Her presence has cooled my hot temper, but a barren numbness has replaced it. I hate this sort of emotion, the profound sense of hopelessness, I prefer the anger. Rage I can deal with, I can turn it into something positive. Sadness makes me weak and vulnerable.

Her arms snake around my neck and I rest my weary head on her shoulders. The sound of the zombies snarling lustfully outside is getting much louder. There's nothing I can do, this place is over. I try to accept this in my heart, but the fear that we're going to lose people is too much to bear. In here, we're protected. I'm not sure of my group's chances out there on the harsh road. They just haven't experienced it yet, and I don't want their first time out there to be fatal.

As Emily pulls away, patting me on the back, I try to adapt the old faithful tactic of imagining that none of this is real and I'm on a film set, but I can't find the enthusiasm for it. This *is* reality; the people that die are lost forever. The zombies outside are actually a real thing and anyone who becomes one can't take off their makeup at the end of the day and return to normal life. Using my imagination as a coping mechanism has been a childish method of getting by. I can't block out my worries in that manner anymore. Something inside of me has irrevocably changed.

I can't let anyone else die. However much I've tried to convince myself that losing my family hasn't bothered me because it was their own fault, I'll never get over that loss. I'll never forgive myself. I can't let the same happen to my new family. I've let people in, I've allowed myself to care, and now I'm paying the price for that mistake. I always said sentiment in the zombie apocalypse gets you killed, but loving these people crept up on me. I didn't notice it happening until it was far too late.

I stuff everything into my backpack, trying not to over-analyse my actions. I've got to fuel myself forward, however I'm feeling. I need to try to prevent my emotions from being the death of me, I know that, I've told myself that so many times, so why do the words feel so hollow now?

I can hear the children talking excitedly between themselves. They have no true idea of the danger we're about to embark on. This is all a big adventure to them, they're probably glad to be getting out of here. Being stuck indoors is no good for boys of their age. Everyone else is talking, but I feel detached, more like I'm having an out of body experience and I'm just watching the scene from somewhere else. I'm just a useless void and I need to snap out of it if I'm going to be any use outside of these four walls.

I attempt to focus my attention; I look intently at every single member of the group, trying to gauge their opinions. All their faces show varying stages of distress and fear, except Pete, who looks oddly relieved. He shoots a smile my way and I can't help my reflex reaction by grinning back. For some reason, the look he gives me makes me feel like we're the only people in this room. The way he's gazing at me makes me feel important, like I *really* matter. I can't fully explain it, even to myself. I feel like he can see into my soul and instead of making me uneasy, the way I'd like it to, I feel a bit flattered by the attention. I hate that. I want to despise him so badly. However irrational my feelings are, I blame him for all the bad things that are currently happening. When I focus on all the problems he's created for me, it's easy to. But when he's looking at me like that, it all melts away.

I drink in his entire appearance again, just like the first time I saw him. Back then I only noticed his looks; I didn't have a clue about his personality. Now that I know him a bit better, his kind, sweet side shines through, making him that much more attractive. I realise then that he's exactly 'my type'—the sort of guy I used to date. I never had a serious boyfriend, of course, we moved about too much, we were never in one place for longer than six months, but I did go on a lot of dates. If I'd met him under any other circumstances, I'm sure I would've been flirting like mad by now.

I shake my head, wishing these thoughts away. I've just allowed them to enter my brain because I'm feeling upset and maudlin. I can't think with anything other than my brain during the zombie apocalypse, I don't want to end up dead because of my feelings for someone else. I'm already too attached to everyone in this group; I can't add romance or love into the mix. That'll finish me off for sure.

My ears suddenly zone in on the conversation Randy is having with Sarah. He's discussing the imminent need for camping material. Panic consumes all of my previous emotions. I can't camp, I refuse. When watching *any* horror film, I always said that the biggest mistake that the characters made is setting foot inside a tent, leaving just a scrap of material between themselves and the monsters outside.

I refuse. I flatly refuse to allow that to be me.

"No, we should find a—" I'm shushed immediately by Randy. He looks at me impatiently like he doesn't have time for my nonsense right now. I'm taken aback by his rudeness; he's never treated me like that before, like an impertinent child. I know we're all stressed but there was absolutely no need for that.

I'm ambushed by hurt and confusion. I almost consider sitting down and refusing to move until he apologises for treating me that way—however bratty and unreasonable that may be—but then Emily slips her hand into mine and a calming sensation rushes over me and I find myself starting to empathise with Randy. This *is* a tense situation, which we all need to work through together. I shouldn't take his snappiness so personally.

"Okay, everyone. Me, Pete, and Alyssa will go first, making a route for Emily and Sarah, who will bring Ben and Leon. Understand?" He says this in an authoritative voice, which none of us can disagree with. He's taking charge, shouldering the responsibility of the decision. Now we just need to make it work.

I watch silently as the doors swing open.

CHAPTER 34

DR. JONES

March 22nd

10:20 a.m.

I can't believe what's happened. I'm in utter shock, but no matter how many times I retest and look over the results, it always spells out the same answer. I've had such a major breakthrough; it hasn't even begun to sink in yet. I don't even know what to do with myself while I process this information.

The thing is, it happened completely by accident. The first time I got the positive result, I wasn't even sure what I'd done. The vial of blood that I'd taken from Jason was changing before my very eyes and all I could do was watch and wait. Then I had to rush through all my scruffy notes that I'd written, ready to write up later if anything of significance occurred.

I've found a cure for cancer!

Well, at least I think I have. It certainly looks that way. Can you believe it? I certainly can't! All the years of research that have gone into it and somehow I've fixed it without even intending to.

I was running some tests using some of the chemicals that I hadn't used yet in previous experiments. I wasn't expecting anything; nothing has happened so far—in fact, I was starting to believe that nothing was ever going to happen. As always, I had a vial of blood from myself—uninfected—and from specimens in varying stages, in this case one, seven, and Jason. This time, I had the idea of creating a vial of 'recently infected' blood by combining mine and Jason's. I had no idea if this was going to be effective, but it's the closest I can get. By the time the specimens are brought to me, *they're already—at minimum—a few hours in. I wanted to see if anything could be done within seconds of infection.*

The blood sample I created was effective, it had exactly the same qualities as all of the other infected samples, but unfortunately it didn't provide any different results to what I've previously seen. All I can conclude is that as soon as AM13 enters your blood stream, it's too late to stop it from transferring all the way into stage three. A point that I've already noted, as depressing a note as it is, nothing I do seems to alter that result.

So almost immediately, the combination of Fluticasone, Infliximab, Erythopoietin and Cisplatin—a combination, as far as I'm currently aware, never seen together—the cancerous cells started disappearing at a rapid rate. Aside from the AM13 virus, Jason's blood was completely clear.

Of course, now I need to figure out how much of that was down to the infection of the AM13 virus. I'm afraid that it could be a lot. I don't want to present the cure just to find out that sufferers need to be infected with another deadly virus first. One that has no aid or solution. For the moment, anyway.

I know this is a detour in my research. It isn't my instructed duty, but it's still something of a miracle. I can't wait to show my findings to the board, at least then all of the criticism will be forced to stop. They can't exactly continue saying I'm doing nothing when I've discovered this cure. The cure for one of the most awful diseases to face humanity before AM13.

I'm sure now that if I can do this, I can tackle the job that I'm supposed to be working on. I'll find a way somehow. I can do it. I can.

3:15 p.m.

I've been called to a meeting with the board in 15 minutes so I'm gathering up all of my notes. I'm actually really excited about this. I'm still trying to figure out how much AM13 impacts on the cure. Without cancerous but uninfected blood, it's challenging. I'm sure this meeting will lead to more assistance on this task. It's so important, I'm sure resources will be found somehow.

I still haven't recovered from the enormity of this. When I think of all the time, effort, and funding that has previously gone into this research, and I've found something of an answer...and quite a simple one at that. Whatever the outcome, it's a start!

5:05 p.m.

I'm speechless. I don't even know how to write all of this down. Where do I begin?

They don't want to know. Not at all. In fact, rather than dispelling the criticism, it became a hundred times worse. Why can't they see what a good thing this is? Even if the research is incomplete, it's a massive step in the right direction.

No, criticism isn't even the word. This time, the threats weren't implied, they were real. Accompanied by violence. A soldier was ordered to hold a knife against my throat.

My breathing was restricted, I started to get dizzy. Words were yelled at me, but I couldn't hear them, my ears had gone fuzzy with fear. Although I've known for a while that the board members are bad people, this is the first time I've had that fact thrust in my face.

My family. I want to know where they are. I suspect now more than ever that the board isn't treating them well. What if they're being held somewhere? Being mistreated? Why didn't I just stick to my original plan and stay with Ashley and Melody throughout all of this? Why did I allow myself to get duped in such a terrible fashion? Questions and emotions are flying though me, making it very difficult to concentrate on anything. I could scream with frustration. I need to get out of here. I need to leave this place. Now. I can't last much longer. I don't know if I can do this anymore.

Fucking hell, what am I doing?

3:00 a.m.

I've calmed down a bit. Now I'm just really upset. I've talked everything through with Jason and he's got me back on the right path. Escape just isn't a viable option. They'll kill me for sure. These people aren't reasonable. I just need to get some form of solution, anything will do. An answer, whatever it may be. Even if the result is incomplete, not fully tested. I need to give them something.

Jason is already looking better after ingesting my solution—it was his idea to take it, I didn't want to force that choice upon him. I couldn't ask him to be my guinea pig, much as it would help my work. I've told him to continue on his cancer medication as it still seems to be slowing down AM13. I don't want to risk losing him over finding the answer to the wrong question. Not when he means as much to me as he does.

Now that my mind is thinking more rationally, I can't stop thinking about the amount of food they had in that boardroom. Their dinner was served to them whilst I was still in there. If I thought I was being served a lot to eat, I was very mistaken. I've never seen such a banquet! I'm sure they don't need that much, do they? It can't have all been eaten. What a waste. You'd think in this situation, rationing supplies would be essential? It was almost disgusting.

I have to assume that they have plans in place. That they don't expect us to be here for too much longer, for them not to be considering too far into the future. I want to know what's happening, but I'm sure I don't have any rights to ask. Especially when I'm viewed in such a negative way. This lack of knowledge is harder to swallow than anything else.

I wish I could continue with my research on the medication I created today, but I know that'll just get me in more trouble. Instead I'm going to leave a sample of my discovery in the back of this notebook complete with detailed instructions—just in case something happens to me. I can't be certain of anything anymore. If I survive, I fully intend to pursue this further, and if I don't, I really hope that someone else does. This could be one of the biggest discoveries of this century if only it's allowed to progress.

If someone finds this work and wants to credit me for my contribution, my name is Dr. Edmond Jones, born 15/12/1985. I graduated from Oxford University in 2007. A quick search online should pull up any more details—I know the university library contains a lot of my previous research data. I would like to be remembered for contributing something to the world, especially after all the struggles I've endured to achieve this.

Especially since I may not get the opportunity to do anything else.

CHAPTER 35

ALYSSA

"There's no way out." The words slip out of my mouth without me even realising I was thinking them. There are more zombies outside than I even considered possible. I hear an audible gasp behind me, someone else is sharing my shocked reaction. I glance over to Randy and Pete, my comrades, and see determination gripping both of their faces. I try to adopt the same stance; this is exactly the sort of excitement I've been crying out for. Another chance to prove myself. I need to shake off all of the negativity that could potentially affect my performance. These people are relying on me. However furiously my heart is pounding, however much fear sits in the pit of my stomach, I need to come through. Emily, Sarah, and the children need me to do this.

"Get back!" Randy yells as the zombies start to pile inside. I don't look behind me to see if they've listened. Instead I move forward, trying to push the infected backwards again. As soon as they invade this space, we'll never make it out. I block out the screaming and shouting going on around me, I need to clear my mind to focus. This is life or death. I *can* do this, I have to.

I keep my awareness levels high even as I plunge my axe into the head of a disgusting crawler. I hadn't seen a zombie missing the bottom half of its body up until this point, so I wasn't expecting it. Its teeth were just about to sink into my ankle when I felt a drip of its saliva hitting my leg. Thank goodness I did or I'd be infected by now.

I glance down, revolted by its remains. Its head almost exploded by the force of my axe and has left a terrible, bloody mess at my feet. An eyeball rolls to the left and dark purple sludge sits on my boots. I feel a rush of queasiness as I realise that it's the zombie's blood. Whatever has been going on inside its body since it turned has created that gross mess I'm standing on. It's amazing how much worse seeing these things in real life really is. I think it's the combination of the sight *and* the smell. I don't think the rotten, burnt out flesh is a scent I'll ever become accustomed to.

They don't stop coming. In fact, they're coming from all angles. There seems to be no end to the undead swarm. Luckily I have Pete and Randy watching my back. I don't know how many times they've saved me, but I've also been doing the same for them. It's so hard to have your eyes everywhere all at once.

* * *

I'm panting, I'm out of breath. I've lost count of how many zombies I've killed. My lovely clean outfit is now covered in blood, pus, mud, and general grime. My hair is dripping with it all. The zombies seem to finally be decreasing in numbers, which is brilliant, because I'm not sure how much fight I have left in me. My arms are thoroughly aching with the constant thrusting.

"Is everyone all right?" The voice breaks through my barrier of fatigue. I nod, unable to speak yet. I notice a flash of Randy running past me and Pete, back inside the church. He must be checking on the others. I hope they hid well and nothing got inside. We *did* make a conscious effort to stop all the zombies entering, but anything could have happened when we weren't aware. I can't think too deeply into this, we still have to fight the final few until they're gone or we're all together and we can run. I hope I have enough energy left to move quickly. I can't help but think of that massive horde I saw a long time ago as soon as I left my house. I wonder if I can run as fast as I did back then.

To my utter relief, everyone eventually exits, looking relatively unharmed. As they leave the church, they start running, and despite my body's screaming protests, I follow suit. We continue until we reach the shopping centre I visited previously—the one where we found Pete. He's gone inside with Randy, searching for camping equipment, while I wait with the others. I keep my mouth shut, even though there's a whole lot I want to say about their stupid plan. I can't suffer a dispute at the moment. I'll just have to cope for now. I've survived outside before and I can do it again, but after tonight I *will* say my piece. I'll argue the logical case; I'll make everyone come around to my way of thinking.

I can do that—I'm supposed to be the heroine of this movie, for goodness sake!

I keep up the silence as they run back outside and we hurry towards the woodland. Everything inside me is telling me that this is definitely the wrong thing to do, but still I don't speak. There isn't any point; everyone is soaking up all of Pete's *'tips'* on how to find a great camping place, so I know no one will want to hear what I have to say. How he's managed to put everyone so far under his spell—except me, of course—is unbelievable.

We find a small opening within the trees and before long, the tents are pitched. Even though the cold is starting to set in, we can't set a fire. That'll announce our location to any zombies in the nearby area. I can hear Randy, Pete, and Sarah discussing the plans for the night, to keep us safe. I'm sure I would be included in this conversation if I chose to be, but I don't want any involvement. I don't want to be responsible for all these terrible decisions being made. I just sit listening, staring at my feet. Times are set for us to keep watch, which we'll do in shifts and in groups of two. I won't be sleeping anyway, so this is no issue for me.

After dinner, the cold becomes too much, so even before the darkness has set in, everyone retires to their tents. Sarah and Randy share with their young children, which leaves me with the choice of bunking with Pete or Emily. An unwelcome fission of nerves settles in my stomach at the prospect of sharing with Pete, and for that exact reason I choose Emily. I can't figure out what it is I feel for Pete, if it's hate or something else, and I don't want to work it out. I don't need any of this confusion. I just need to focus on survival.

It's been a long time since I've been able to have a decent chat with Emily, so I find myself really glad of the time alone. We talk for hours and I eventually steer the conversation to the topic I wish to discuss. This new development in our adventure has brought up a lot of feelings that I've tried very hard to suppress. Loss. It started at the church, and hasn't left my mind, even during the fight.

I discuss my family, reminiscing over past times. I never thought I'd be able to do this—but with Emily, I just feel comfortable. I can feel the tears threatening to come out, but I carry on talking regardless. I can't keep acting as if they didn't exist or never mattered. It's hard enough to grieve or recover from things in the zombie apocalypse—you just don't have the time; you're left in a constant limbo—so when I *can* organise my feelings, I suppose I should. I feel like a balloon being let down a little at a time as I speak. I've been so full up of all of this tight, difficult emotion and it's such a release to finally be able to let it all out.

I leave out the details of their deaths; it's obvious that they're no longer here, so it's not something that *needs* to be discussed. I particularly don't want to go into details of Lexi's demise; I think that'll really push me over the edge into despair. I know I'll have to eventually, but now just isn't the time. I don't want Emily to regard me differently, to look at me in an altered way. She may not understand that I did what I had to do. She hasn't been faced with that situation yet. She views the zombies in a unique way, an academic way—obviously she sees the threat, but her mind just draws unique conclusions.

When my voice catches and I can't continue with my story, Emily takes over and tells me about her father. I already know about their time after the zombies came, so she also goes into details of her life beforehand. It quickly becomes apparent that she isn't as religious as her parents as she regales the time of her teenage rebellion with an undertone of joy. She always hated growing up under such strict rules, so as she reached adolescence, she went far too over the top, trying to separate herself from her family. Drinking, partying all night, even recreational drugs. I'm shocked, I had her down as such a prude, but it seems her youth has been far more exciting and experimental than mine. I guess with no solid friendships, I didn't have anyone to do all of this with.

Then my astonishment goes even further as she tells me the tale of trying to hide all of her girlfriends from her dad, for fear of serious retribution, because homosexuality was frowned upon in his church. This stuns me into silence. My eyebrows shoot up so high, they might even have left my face for a second. *Emily's a lesbian.* I'd have never in a million years guessed that. As she continues, unaware of my reaction, I start to feel uncomfortable at our close proximity. By picking Emily over Pete have I given her the wrong message? I shuffle about, more obviously that I would like. My cheeks feel like they are on fire, and I stutter, trying to discreetly change the topic. She looks confused, and more than a little hurt.

"You know I'm not going to pounce on you in the middle of the night, right?"

"Of course, I—"I start to laugh awkwardly. I don't want to make this situation more prickly than it already is.

"Because it's quite obvious that you aren't into girls…"She leaves that sentence hanging in the air and I nod along silently. I feel oddly disappointed, which is completely the wrong emotion for this moment. I'm glad it's obvious, I wouldn't want any uncertainty.

No, I'm definitely straight, as heterosexual as they come. The tingly feeling that's inside of me right now is just confusion and shock. I mean, I *do* connect with Emily, but that is just because we've been forced together in awful circumstances. My feelings for her are purely platonic. I would never think of her as anything more, I couldn't. That isn't me at all.

But as we say our goodnights and Emily shuts her eyes, all in can think about is her breath on my face.

CHAPTER 36

DR. JONES

March 24th

6:15 a.m.

Things are getting weirder by the second. I still haven't worked out how to process any of it yet. I haven't slept in about 36 hours, so not only is my mind reeling with the new information its received, exhaustion is contributing an adverse effect.

It all started yesterday lunchtime, when my meal was delivered. As I've probably commented in an earlier note, the amount of food I've been receiving has been more than substantial. In fact, it's been brilliant because I've been able to share it with the specimens that are in stage one and occasionally stage two when they're still up for eating. Of course, Jason has benefitted immensely. But yesterday I was simply served a few crackers and a tiny lump of cheese. The guy that delivered it to me had put it down and left before I had time to question him. I don't usually leave my work to talk to anyone that comes down here unless I'm forced to, but it was quite obvious that he rushed so as not to get involved with my fury.

At first I was confused. I didn't want to contact the board and complain. That seemed a bit of an unsuitable reaction when resources could very well be scarce. Then I remembered the feast I'd seen only a couple of days before in that boardroom. Things can't be that dire if they're eating and wasting food to that extent. I started to moan idly to Jason about it while internally trying to decide on my next move. That's when it all came spilling out. But before I get to that I just want to comment that I've *realised the lack of food is my punishment for not acting exactly on their instructions. Because I stumbled across another solution, I'm having my luxuries stripped away.*

This is when, for the very first time, I learned the truth of what's really happening outside the confines of this building. As I only know it from Jason's perspective, I'm going to write it down here as his story.

Jason arrived here approximately the same date as I did. He was alone—he doesn't mention any family and I don't ask. Subjects like that can be very sensitive in these times. They didn't land in an airport, it was a large field, which they were left in for hours before anything was organised. He believes that we are on a small European island somewhere, but no one has been given concrete information about this. He's heard rumours in camp that it's an island that didn't receive much tourism, which is why it was never hit by AM13. He also heard that there is a large wall surrounding the area, but doesn't know how much truth there is in that. It could all simply be hearsay.

At this point I'd just like to mention that Jason knows less about the men in charge than I do. He's as unsure as me as to what gave them the power, although he assumes at least some of them are government members.

After a while, they were all led to a massive, derelict campsite. Although there was underlying grumbling, no one outwardly complained because it was obvious that no one had much choice—these people had battled through the streets of the UK to get to their airports, just the same as me. This was a much better option than that at least.

The food portions have always been meagre—Jason was surprised about what I get in here. He'd be furious if he saw what I did in the boardroom—and it's unbearably freezing cold. They're living under incredibly strict rules; policed by 'muscle men' who don't appear to have any regulations on the amount of force they're allowed to use to keep things under control. These are also the *people who weed out any signs of infection and bring them in here to me.*

Here is where I asked Jason where his bite came from. He believes that someone snuck in an infected person onto the plane as there have been random flare-ups of the virus within camp. He got bitten by a young boy hours before he was ushered down here—I wonder if this was James Max. Any one that fights against being brought here is shot. There are no second chances. Families are torn apart in a terribly violent fashion.

This led to dissatisfaction slowly turning into full-blown angry riots. The resolve is obviously awful and everyone is now terribly frightened. Just as Jason was bitten, the living situation was beginning to become excruciating. He 'dreads to think how awful it must be now.' When he was brought into this underground laboratory he was shocked by how warm and spacious it is. He has often wondered why they haven't made this the living space. Of course, the food portions have been a bit of a sticking point as well.

Luckily he caught on quickly how little power and control I have, or things could've gotten very awkward.

Life in here has actually been preferable for Jason. He's felt much safer since he became infected. I can't even begin to get my head around that one. It must be god awful for that to be the case. It's hell in here.

Of course I had to ask why he'd kept all that information from me until now, I've complained enough about my fears for Ashley and Melody. But that was the exact reason he gave for keeping me in the dark. He didn't want to frighten me and send me way off course. He knew what this knowledge could do to me and he didn't want to distract me from my research. Not for selfish reasons, but he knows that I have to do this to get out. He knows the board will kill me if I don't.

But it has now gotten too far. He couldn't keep it in any longer. He needed to put the fire under my belly to get me motivated again. I understand. I do, but it doesn't make any of it any easier to digest.

I can't focus, I feel sick. I thought writing all of this down would help me make some sort of sense of it, but it hasn't. I'm more confused than ever. I need to see my family. This won't do anymore. I can't do anything, I won't. They're on my mind all the time. I must be able to do something? I'd give up my position if I thought that would help but I know with a sure fire certainty that it won't. If I beg, plead, bow down to their requirements, surely they can't deny me my family any longer? I know that I've already stepped way outside my boundary to allow that to happen, and it didn't, but I need to try again.

I can't carry on like this. I can't take anymore.

I have never felt so low before. I have a weird sense of loss, a pit of unease lying flatly in the bottom of my stomach. I shouldn't be writing this sort of thing really, these notes are supposed to be emotion-free. A scientific journal. But I guess it gives a *bigger picture of the events that are going on.*

Or maybe I just need the sense of relief that comes from getting it off of my chest.

CHAPTER 37

ALYSSA

Eventually Randy pops his head into our tent, breaking the one-sided tension. It's mine and Emily's turn to keep watch for two hours, after which Sarah will take over with Pete. Apart from Randy, we decided to stick in twos with one 'fighter' in each pairing, so that we can watch each other's backs. I push myself up carefully, but glad to have a valid reason to remove myself from the uncomfortable situation. I've barely slept a wink since Emily's revelation, whereas she has been merrily snoring away, unaware of the effect she's had on me.

I climb out solo, enjoying the sensation of the cool breeze brushing my skin. I need some time by myself out in the open air to clear my mind and organise my thoughts. More close proximity to Emily will just cloud my judgement further. I don't want to experience these strange feelings. I couldn't bear it if things became awkward between us; I love my friendship with Emily—she's the closest companion I've ever had. This zombie apocalypse has forced us to become close very quickly, and for someone like me, that's amazing.

The thing is, deep down, I do know why I feel so strange but I'm nowhere near ready to admit it to myself yet. I force my thoughts back towards Pete. As much as he annoys me, I feel like we had a real connecting moment back at the church before we embarked on this ludicrous mission. I know I instantly dismissed it, for very good reason. But now, in the light of this new emotional turmoil, I feel the need to revisit it. Why have I not fixated on that occurrence? Why was it so easy to push it from my mind, readily accepting that nothing would ever come between us, but thoughts of Emily become more enticing and tantalising?

Maybe it's just the pressure of losing the church. I've been feeling all over the place since then. I barely even feel like myself anymore. Maybe it's just because Emily's revelation has shocked me. I guess finding out that my pre-conceived notions about her being buttoned-up and very serious were way off has made me reconsider everything. I'm obviously just transferring this into baffling thoughts. Thoughts that far overstep the boundaries of friendship.

I tug at the ends of my hair, trying to push the images of Emily's plump red lips, long pale matted hair, and deep chocolate brown eyes out of my mind. I've *got* to stop it. I need to get out of my head. I'm letting my imagination run wild. It's the damn zombie apocalypse doing this to me. It's a weird life-or-death situation and I'm clinging onto people in a way that's much different than what I'm used to. After losing my family and spending so much time alone, it was bound to have some sort of negative impact on me.

I just need to carry on as normal; all these feelings will soon pass me by. I'll just forget tonight, pretend it never happened, and all will be fine. Really, with flesh-eating zombies roaming around the country, a little bit of mixed emotion is a tiny and insignificant problem. I need to remember that I'm out here camping—my very worst nightmare. I need to ensure I survive so that tomorrow I can tackle Randy and Pete.

It isn't long before Sarah comes to join me, my watch turn already over. As Pete hasn't woken up yet, I decide to sit with her for a while, prolonging the time before I have to return to the confines of the tent. We talk about everything and nothing. Mostly tales about our lives before AM13. I'm surprised to find out how cool she actually is. She's much more laid back out here in this one-on-one conversation. I can clearly see how she has slotted into the 'caring motherly' role that our group really needs, but in reality she is so much more than that. It's nice to be able to feel close to her, knowing how far she'd disconnected from everyone.

After a while, Pete arrives, bleary-eyed and yawing, and I can no longer find a reason to stay. As I wander back to the tent, fatigue starts to get to me and I'm actually asleep before my head hits the pillow. Obviously sitting alone was the best thing I could have done, clearing out any unwelcome thoughts. I never thought I'd be able to rest out here, putting my life in the hands of others. In the past, that would have never happened.

In the end, I'm woken up by everyone else rising. I'm shocked to see that morning has arrived, at one point it felt like that would never happen. Emily barely speaks one word to me over breakfast and again I find myself desperately trying to figure out what I did wrong. She was asleep during my hours of contemplation and I thought she didn't really notice my initial reaction. Have I somehow given the impression that I'm just another judgmental person? How can I convey to her that couldn't be further from the truth, without accidentally giving across another incorrect notion?

As soon as the food has been eaten, Pete starts up again about our movements for the day. I try to see if anyone else is starting to find the concept of this lifestyle as insane as I do, but to my intense disappointment, people are either barely listening or showing signs of bare acceptance. Now is the time to speak up. If I don't right now I'll be forced to suffer another night in a tent.

"How about we—"

"Come on, Alyssa, now isn't the time for arguing," Randy interrupts me again. I can't work out why he suddenly has such a negative attitude towards me. I thought we got on fine, I never noticed any disapproval from him before. As I glare towards him, I suddenly notice how exhausted he looks. Maybe he thinks I'm just trying to cause trouble, I don't know what would give him that impression. Instead, I'm spurred on by the prospect that I just *know* my suggestion is better.

"No, I don't want to cause issues. I just want to at least discuss my idea. Give everyone another option from this constant wandering. It won't do us any good in the long run." My pleading eyes go unnoticed but no one interrupts. "*If* we could find somewhere safe, somewhere much more suitable than the church, couldn't we at least attempt to stay there?" I look around to see everyone is intently listening. Finally I'm being considered again. I need to run this home while I have everyone's attention. "We're going to need a few days' rest eventually, this is going to become tiring quickly. If any signs of us becoming surrounded arise, of course we'll move on and try somewhere else. Camping won't be ideal forever; we have to consider elements outside of the zombies. Cold, for instance." I find myself gesturing wildly as if I'm really getting into this role. "And we mustn't give up hope. I don't want to accept that England is lost forever. We need to at least *believe* that one day someone will come back for us. Surely they're going to want this country to be inhabitable again at some point? We know for a fact that the human race hasn't died out, this isn't your typical Hollywood zombie apocalypse film, this is real life. A life where the government has a contingency plan, we just happened to miss it. They'll come back; we just need to keep on going until then. Finding somewhere safe to stay will help us succeed."

I've gone off on a slight tangent, taking this monologue a bit too far. I've started spouting things that are only a minute possibility as if I'm utterly convinced that they're true. White lies aside, it seems to be working. I spot flickers of positivity and it drives home just how fed up everyone has been. Even me. I always had abstract fantasies about myself thriving in this sort of situation. I envisioned myself becoming a better person simply through living in my own horror film. I thought anything was better than the hollow, shallow life I was surviving in before. But it's a lot tougher than I could have ever suspected. I may have formed much stronger bonds with people, I've actually been in the same place long enough to find friends, but I don't think I've thrived. I don't think I'm a better person. I think all of this has highlighted how weak I really am. Maybe not physically—I have fought well against the zombies—but mentally. It's brought to light how little I really know about myself. I don't think I've ever been a full person with an entire personality. I've never sat in one place long enough to know a single thing about myself.

A small voice pushes this upsetting revelation aside. Leon pipes up in a tiny voice. "I agree with Alyssa. I liked it better inside than out here. It's scarier than I thought it would be." Ben nods emphatically beside him. I smile warmly at them both. I've not had a great deal to do with the children; I've been trying to include myself in the 'adult' section of the group. I'm so pleased that they've spoke up for themselves, and not just because they're on my side. They deserve to be considered in our decisions as much, if not more, than the rest of us.

Fortunately Sarah is immediately swayed by her son's words and I can see Randy being pulled in every direction too. I keep silent, knowing that I no longer need to contribute. It won't be long before the majority agrees with me.

"Yeah actually, Mum, I agree with Alyssa too. Camping isn't as safe as being inside a building. Maybe if we compromise and move between buildings every few days, we can be safer. Plus, we can always keep our eye out for other survivors. We know there must be others." Emily's words are unexpected. I thought she was angry at me for some reason, but maybe she is smart enough to realise that this isn't about me and her. The logic she provides sways everyone onto the right choice. Even Pete can't find disagreement with her words.

As we walk, I start to think about something else Emily said. Other survivors. We still haven't found E. This is bound to change that, whoever it is must still be in the area somewhere. We've just *got* to find E now. I pull the battered piece of paper out of my pocket. The words are illegible now but I have them memorised. Plus the writing on that wall has been committed to my memory. Now that I know I've gotten my way with our living arrangements, I start to obsess over where E might be now.

CHAPTER 38

ETHAN

Clare.
Clare.
Clare.

I'm back at her townhouse. I finally got here. I finally managed to get myself to do what needed to be done, and she's not even here.

All those days, weeks of persuading myself that there was no better end than dying alongside the love of my life—even if it *did* mean getting that disease—and it was all for nothing.

I don't know if *I* left the door open as I ran away last time, giving her the ability to escape, or if someone else has been here. All I know is that my world has fallen out from beneath me. I'm sitting at the bottom of her stairs, thinking her name over and over again. I'm probably rocking back and forth like a crazy person…but who cares? There isn't exactly anyone around to judge me!

I just…I don't know what to do now. I've been

focused so long on this one goal, and now I have nothing. If Clare isn't here, then I have *no idea* where to even begin looking for her—that's just an impossible task.

I keep desperately wishing that this would all end and life would go back to normal. I miss having a life. Anything is better than this. But if it did return, would I even be able to survive? Look at me, I'm a mess. Too scared to do anything. I was always bad, but now I'm incurable. Even if I thought there was a hope for the human race to overcome this, I don't believe that there's a hope for me anymore.

Maybe I should just get it over and done with, and just *really* kill myself this time. No more waiting until I'm brave enough, or it feels right. Just get it damn well done already. It's not like I have anything left to live for. I have no one—the entire country is empty! I've already accepted that I'm going to die; I came here ready to do it, so maybe I should stick to that plan and do it anyway.

It doesn't really matter—I'm dying anyway.

I haven't eaten for…I don't even know how long. I'm exhausted, skinny, and finding life harder than ever. Death would be easier than this!

But how will I do it?

Just as my mind comes up with hundreds of different concepts of how I could end my miserable little existence, another thought pops into my mind. A woman—one that I haven't given a passing thought for a little while now. The one that's still stuck inside my home. Whatever mistakes I made with Clare won't have happened here. I was *sure* to lock her in.

I may not be able to die with the woman I love, but surely it'd be better to die with my one remaining family member.

Leah.

She came to me for a reason. I had no idea what that was at the time, but now I do. I'm far too cowardly to *actually* kill myself. I can think about it as an abstract concept, but actually *doing* it—that will never happen.

A spark of excitement flickers deep inside me at the thought of having an answer. It may be a crazy one, but right now, I think I am crazy. I jump upright off the stairs and move towards the door. Now that I know what I'm doing, I can push all of the agonising pain that's racking through my body to one side. I can even live along my doomsday voice, because what it's screaming at me is what I want to do.

Leah, I'm coming, Leah!

CHAPTER 39

DR. JONES

March 30th

1:25 p.m.

Cough.

Sniff.

Sneeze.

These sounds have started to haunt me. I can no longer ignore the fact that Jason is starting to finally display the early signs of AM13. I've been pointedly ignoring the festering wound on his forearm. I've been trying to act like it isn't even there, even though it's been difficult to take no notice of the fact that it's been getting more disgusting as time has gone by. Even though

I haven't had a specimen long enough to see the deterioration occurring as much as I would like to, I can see it in this area. It's black, rotting, and the smell is horrendous. Even though I never comment on it, I can see how much difficulty Jason is having using it. It's becoming a useless limb.

I can't help but wonder how much of this is to do with the lack of cancerous cells he now has in his body. Have I brought on the effects of AM13 much quicker by taking away the disease that seemed to be blocking it? He's still taking his medication, but I don't think it's holding the virus off any longer. I can't help but worry that he will progress through the three stages much quicker having avoided them for so long—and it's all my fault.

I've worked with all the medications I noted previously, I've run test after test, but still haven't come up with something satisfactory. Isolating each chemical hasn't provided me with a link to which one was holding off the AM13 virus. I'm not entirely sure if Jason has just been lucky. AM13 is so unpredictable, that's as much of a possibility as anything else, unfortunately.

Using my professional head, I have come up with another—possibly very substandard—theory. Using Jason's wound; I wonder how long it would take the infected to literally die out. Maybe, without any opportunity to spread the virus further—or a 'food source,' of course I still can't be 100% on my previous notes—maybe the infected will not be able to survive for long. It came to me as more of a passing thought, but the more I obsess over the concept, the more I realise it could be correct.

I can't see the board being pleased with this idea. It offers no miracle cure or antidote. In fact, all it suggests is that we wait it out until the UK could possibly be much safer. It's a tough grey area too because judging by the variation in the specimens, it could take a long time for them to all deteriorate into non-existence. Then of course, without the knowledge of what brought this virus into being, the possibility of another flare-up will be an ever present threat.

Part of me wonders if someone somewhere does know where AM13 came from. I would have thought that a lot of time, money, and energy would be put into finding this out. It's quite possible that it could be some sort of nuclear weapon. Maybe this is World War Three and none of us have worked that out yet. At any rate, I haven't noticed too much concern about this topic from the board members. Why aren't they bothered? It's so curious.

~~Maybe they started it to get to where they are now.~~

Ignore that last remark, I'm allowing my emotions and imagination to get in the way of my work again.

4:15 p.m.
16. Kevin Hall, 32, Factory Worker
5"9', black hair, dark brown eyes.
Previous medical condition—diabetes.

His wife and father are in the camp.

He was brought in during the latter stages of stage two. He's now in stage three. His body is already showing signs of the deterioration I've seen in Jason. I wonder if they've all shown this, but I'm just noticing it now as it's something that I've decided to focus on?

17. Joanna Scott, 39, Magazine Editor.

5"2', red hair, green eyes.

No previous medical conditions.

I have no knowledge of any family left in camp. One of the soldiers has implied that she's related to one of my previous specimens, but I'm not sure how much truth there is in that.

She's in stage one, but incredibly ill from the flu symptoms. She's the first I've seen so affected by this. I'll need to keep an eye on her to see if this not only affects her development, but her condition after reaching stage three.

18. 'John Smith'

I have no information on this specimen.

Nothing was brought with him. I can only assume that he's in his early twenties. His features are now indistinguishable due to the damage his body has received. He appears to have been in stage three for a long time now—I don't know why I didn't receive him earlier. I can't continue to question the mysteries of what goes on around here—it causes me more trouble than it's worth.

Whilst the soldiers were in here delivering my new specimens, they attempted to take away specimen fourteen. I managed to convince them to leave her—after all she's now the 'oldest' specimen I have. I wish I'd managed to hold onto some of the others, especially those twins. They were showing some interesting signs, but I let them go because I hadn't even considered my latest theory at that point. Once they'd delved into the latter part of stage three, I lost interest. They no longer held any merits for me. That's where my main mistake has been.

But now I'm going to use specimen fourteen, and possibly some of the newer entries, to see if I'm right. Apologies to Rachel Lawrence and her family for using her body for science in such a way. It's cruel to prolong her agony, but she could give me the greatest clue to all of this.

8:30 p.m.

Something terrible just happened. Something I don't even want to note down because of the horrible implications that come along with it.

Jason just lost a game of chess to me.

Seeing it written down like that doesn't even begin to display the catastrophic nature behind the sentence. I feel the need to explain this information further.

As I've previously noted, I've been playing chess with Jason during the evenings to help me wind down from all of this intense research. Rather than being a distraction, the change of activity has been helping with my work. Jason is an exceptional chess player and this has been a running joke between us. He hasn't lost to me once. I've *taken it all in good humour, enjoying the motion of playing much more than the competition, but this loss has brought everything to light. Everything that I suspected has shone through.*

His brain function is starting to fail him.

When I knew that the tables were beginning to turn and the odds were working in my favour, I started to study him intently. He looks terrible. Much worse than when he was inflicted with a combination of cancer and AM13. He's dying before my very eyes and I've failed him because I haven't worked out a way to save him.

His blood will be on my hands.

I need to get out of here. I've got to find a way before I end up insane. I fear that losing Jason on top of everything else will strip me of the little sanity I have left.

4:30 a.m.

Is this what depression feels like? I've studied it at some point in my education, but trying to remember it now just brings back fuzzy memories of textbooks and long terminology. That's the problem with learning, until you fully experience something first hand, you can never truly understand. I'm sitting at my desk and I don't want to move ever. If I died right now, I wouldn't care. Not for myself anyway. Of course I couldn't be so selfish for the impact it could have on Ashley and Melody. But if I only had myself to consider, I'd happily end it all.

Why am I even here? What's the point of bothering at all?

I'm watching specimen eighteen and I'm actually jealous of his lack of mental problems. Sure physically he's a mess, but he hasn't got any troubles weighing on his shoulders anymore. All of that brain function is no longer active. He's got it far easier now. I've been trying to imagine what his life was like before, who he might have been, but I can't turn the jealousy off long enough to care.

I'm done. I think it's obvious that I'm done.

CHAPTER 40

ALYSSA

While I'm on a roll with my good ideas being met with positivity, I suggest to Randy that we get a car. That way we can drive around, trying to locate somewhere safe and suitable for the time being, to save wearing ourselves out unnecessarily. There's no argument against that, surely?

Of course I was wrong. Pete, put out by my newfound respect, just *has* to disagree. "It'll lead the infected to wherever we're going. They'll follow the noise."

Not about to be stopped, I continue. "Okay then, how about *someone* takes a car, finds a good place, then we can walk to it after? I think I saw in a film once someone leaving the car with the music blaring and it took all of the zombies way off course!" I'm excited by this memory. I'm pleased by my ingenious scheme.

"Well, there might not be any need to go *that* far, but I think you have the basic idea right, Alyssa." I almost want to stick my tongue out at Pete as Randy agrees with me, but I can't allow myself to be so immature. I can still sense that I need to prove my worth. I wonder if the competitive edge will ever dispel between us.

Before I can speak again, Randy is making plans. "Me and Sarah will go and find a car to have a look around, you lot stay here. Alyssa, Emily, and Pete are in charge, boys, so you must do anything they tell you. Don't forget how dangerous it is out here, okay?" Their pale, drawn faces suggest that they're frightened enough without this being encouraged. "Please don't move unless of course you have to. Maybe we should make the Plan B meeting place the shopping centre? I know it's quite far from here but we all know where it is." We all murmur in agreement, desperately hoping that it doesn't come to that. I don't want to have a mad dash that far, having such responsibility for the boys' lives. The last time I was in charge of a child it didn't end so well, although I doubt I'll be disobeyed here. The boys are much better behaved than Lexi—they know what's at stake.

We sit in an awkward silence after they go. The boys are too tense to talk and there's a weird atmosphere between the rest of us and I have no idea why. Well, I guess I know where Pete's animosity has come from. I've stripped him of all of his power by belittling his idea of constant movement. But why Emily is so mad, I don't know.

"Maybe we should just talk about what's bothering you, Pete. Sitting here angry isn't great. Don't you think we have enough to worry about?" I take the coward's way out and attempt to tackle the easy problem first.

"I'm not angry, Alyssa. I'm just concerned, I suppose. I feel uneasy about stopping. Especially after what happened at the church." He shuts his mouth before anything else can come spilling out. I know there's so much more to his feelings, but the way his jaw is clamped shut I know he isn't going to reveal it anytime soon. He's obviously experienced a lot more than any of us know, but I can't push him to open up. He has to do it in his own time, if at all. I guess for some people, reliving loss and awful memories isn't at all helpful. It may remain a mystery to the rest of us, but everyone has to be able to make their own choices. It's not up to me to force information out of anyone.

After a slight deliberation, I turn to Emily. Using a much softer tone, I start to question her. "Are you okay, Em? You don't seem—"

Water fills her eyes as she turns to face me with a weak smile plastered across her face. She nods tightly, also refusing to open her mouth. Unsatisfied by either of their feeble answers, I turn to the children and try to coax chatter out of them—anything to disperse the awful quiet. I finally manage it by asking them which superhero they thought would be best in the zombie apocalypse. They start to argue over which super powers would be most useful and I sit back, pleased that we no longer have to endure silence.

The others don't move or speak. They continue sitting in their tense positions, bursting with words they won't allow to spill out. I can't bear it so I continually wander around, keeping a look out for zombies. I can't believe how lucky we've been, sitting still and not encountering any yet. It could mean something, couldn't it? Maybe something has happened that we aren't yet aware of.

* * *

Time seems to fly past and soon Randy and Sarah are rushing back to us, panting and head to toe in blood and grime. It looks like they've had a much worse time than us, completely dismissing my optimistic thoughts that someone has come back to kill off all of the infected. Before I allow my brain to consider why we got so lucky, Randy speaks.

"We've found somewhere." My heart lifts as he continues, trying to catch his breath. This is fantastic news, this could solve everything. "It's a risk, so we'll need to approach it carefully. We looked for as long as we could but obviously the noise of the car brought a lot of infected with us. As you can probably tell, it was a struggle getting back here." He gestures to the mess that covers him. "It's an RAF base, so of course going there is incredibly illegal—I'm not too sure how much that matters at the moment—but it's *very* well protected. There's a massive electrical fence surrounding it. It probably won't be on, but it's something." I stand up at this point, already sold on the idea and wanting to move immediately. "I imagine it's got a lot of what we need already there, food in particular—"

"Let's just go, it sounds perfect!" I interrupt. If it's out of town it'll probably take a while to get there, and we need to arrive before dark to avoid another night out in the open. No one else speaks, but to my utter pleasure, they all comply by getting up and starting to move. Things are finally coming together and working out.

* * *

We walk for hours. The entire trip has been silent. I think everyone is full of anticipation because we're walking into the unknown. I'm not feeling that way at all, I'm just distracted and constantly on the lookout for E. I'm certain, with all this distance we're covering, that we will eventually find some sort of clue as to E's whereabouts. Of course the mystery person might not have survived this long, but my instincts tell me that isn't the case.

This keeps me focused the entire journey, meaning I don't allow myself to succumb to the fatigue that's trying desperately to drag me down. If I didn't have these thoughts circling around in my brain, I'm not entirely convinced if I would have made it in one piece! I have no idea how the boys are coping so damn well!

Finally, Randy announces that we're almost there, and everyone lets out a collective sigh of relief. Even Pete seems pleased that we'll have somewhere to stop soon.

Then, my gaze sets upon it, and I smile to myself. It's absolutely perfect!

CHAPTER 41

DR. JONES

April 3rd

10:25 a.m.

Specimen fourteen is showing some interesting developments. No, actually I think that might be the wrong words. She is simply diminishing in the way that I suspected she would. Her motivation levels have waned to practically nothing. Occasionally, if I get too close to her enclosure and she gets a whiff of my uninfected scent, or if I accidentally make a lot of noise, she'll get up and resume hammering against the glass, growling, moaning, and spitting with what can only be described as rage. This will last for a few hours before she appears to simply give up or forget what she was doing and slumps back to the floor, in the same comatose state as before.

Her body is falling apart. Literally. Chunks of rotten, blackened flesh have been falling off of her. A lot of her insides are now visible and none of them are sitting where they should be. It's uncomfortable to look at. She's slowing down more and more each moment. I'm certain that she's becoming a whole lot weaker. I'm very excited by this development; it's the first step in a positive direction that I've come across in terms of AM13. However, it's difficult to test this further at this stage because none of my previous research has looked into this area at all. I'll just have to keep a close eye on Rachael and see how she continues to deteriorate. This is the closest thing I've had to an answer and I'm determined to follow through with it. Even if it is the 'wrong' answer, it's something.

Something is better than nothing, right?

I have given specimen seventeen a sample of the cancer drugs that Jason was originally taking. She was the only subject that I could possibly try this on, even though she was deep into the first stage of infection. I need to keep the other two specimens as they are to confirm anything that I discover from specimen fourteen. If I had more specimens, I'd continue on with this path, but I don't, and there is no guarantee I'll receive anymore. In fact, from a non-scientific point of view, I'd much rather I didn't. I'd like to minimise the suffering as much as I can.

I didn't have high hopes for this medication slowing down the infection in seventeen, but I had to try. I suspect that it had as much to do with cancer as the drugs Jason was taking. Of course, this is another grey area. As far as I'm aware, Jason is the only specimen I've had who was suffering from cancer. All this has shown is that my assumption was correct. Joanna progressed onto stage two in record time. She is now in *stage three. ~~I could almost think that the medication sped the process up for her.~~ Sorry, I'm trying to only write things down that I'm certain about, or at least that I think are correct in my personal opinion. I don't want this entire record to be a mismatch of guesses, but without the correct equipment, knowledge, and variation of specimens, I have to simply do my best.*

So now I'll just continue to monitor Joanna's progress as I'm doing with the others.

2:15 p.m.

Jason has finally reached the second stage of infection. He hasn't said anything, but he doesn't need to. I can just see the agony plastered across his face. As soon as he refused a game of chess, I just knew. Even his loss didn't prevent him from wanting to play. This is pain, pure and simple. His skin is greying, his tongue is turning white. All the signs are there. It's bad, really bad.

He's still fully coherent and a lot more

alert than any of the other specimens have been during this period, which makes it much more unbearable to watch. Jason's body seems to have a much higher pain threshold, which isn't working in his favour. His arm has been rendered useless. I wouldn't be surprised if his hand eventually falls off—I know that's a pretty horrific thought, but it's what I can see in front of my very eyes. It's black, it stinks of rot, of gone off meat, of decay. The tendons are stretching to almost breaking point. The entire limb looks worse by itself than any of the previous specimens I've seen. It's as if that part of him has been in stage three for months, and the rest of him is simply catching up. Maybe this is what I would've seen had I kept the others here. Maybe it's what I will see in the coming days with fourteen. It's not a wonderful thought; in fact, looking at it makes me doubt that the victims will die. Jason seems to continue on just fine, even if his hand/arm is suffering.

I hate writing this down about my friend,

as if he isn't a human being, but simply something that should be monitored. I'm watching him die, and instead of being able to grieve, I'm documenting the process. It's insane, all of it.

I can't watch this. I can't stand seeing Jason go through what all of the others have. I can't bear the thought of him in stage three, hammering on the glass of his enclosure, unable to recognise me or remember any of our friendship. I keep imagining it and even the thought is unbearable.

I'll have to get out of here before then.

3:45 a.m.

Something so terrible just happened. So awful that I need to write it down just so I don't forget the earth shattering fear that I'm experiencing right now. My heart is racing and my hand is still shaking, so I'll get this written down the best way that I can.

I was woken up by a humongous crashing

sound, which blended in with the nightmare I was having in a terrifying way. My heart sank. I just knew that sound meant something awful—when does it not? I could feel it deep inside my chest. To make it worse, it was pitch black, the darkest I've ever experienced. The electricity generator must have cut out at some point during the night. I started to panic, I mean really panic. Something was obviously going on and I couldn't even see as far as the end of my nose. I'm not too proud to admit that I sat gripping onto the edge of my sheet, ears straining for any new noises for quite some time.

As soon as I ascertained that it was safe enough for me to move, I crept into the laboratory. I had to feel my way forward, my eyes just wouldn't adjust to the blackness. I whispered Jason's name, wanting to check he was okay. It's not that I didn't care about any of the other specimens; I just knew that Jason was the only one in any condition to answer me. At least, he had been.

I was met by silence. I started to feel incredibly sick, I was sure that noise would have woken him up too, so for him not to answer me was very strange. I started to assume the worst, the way your mind does when you're put in a frightening situation. I became certain that he'd blasted through the stages at great haste and was now deeply into the third stage. Lost to me before I could even say goodbye.

I kept moving on, trying to position myself outside his enclosure so I could glean a better impression of what was happening. Growling noises seemed to be emanating from every angle, I wasn't even sure if they were real, or still part of the nightmare I'd been having.

The lights flickered on and off rapidly. Someone was obviously trying to get the power up and running, and wasn't doing a particularly good job of it. During this time, two horrifying facts came to life. The first was that Jason's door was wide open. The *second was a trail of blood leading from his enclosure towards the bathroom.*

My presumptions were correct. Jason was no more.

I didn't feel sad. I didn't even feel scared. I didn't feel anything, just a numbness that kept my feet frozen to the spot. My mouth ran dry and I felt like my throat was beginning to close—I don't know how else to describe it.

Then there was more noise. Shuffling, wheezing, inhuman sounds which just confirmed all of my worst fears. My fingers began to throb with the tension. My legs moved of their own accord. My brain wanted to run far away in the opposite direction, but as that wasn't an available option, I pushed myself forward.

I tried to prepare myself for what I was going to see. I warned myself that this could quickly turn nasty. I knew I could get bitten, I was perfectly aware that was a high possibility. I forced myself to imagine killing Jason, because I knew I might have to. I desperately didn't want to fight, I didn't want it to come down to that, but still I continued to move.

It turns out that I didn't have enough time to fully consider all of my options because the next time I looked up, he was there, right in front of me.

He had his back turned to me at first, but I could still see the blood dripping from him. It was blackening and coagulating. By this point, the lights had returned to normal. In my terror I hadn't noticed the moment they'd stopped flickering. I pushed my back against the wall, trying to hide myself, my breaths were heavy and fast. This moment was about to change everything. I knew that nothing would ever be the same again.

Then, movement. I knew it was happening, it was all over. A single tear fell from my eye as I knew Jason was fully infected and about to pass it on to me.

"Hi."

The sound of his voice quickly knocked me out of my stupor. That simple greeting *shocked me to my core and filled me with relief all at the same time. I lost control of my legs and fell to the ground, dizzy with conflicting emotions.*

Jason wasn't confused about my behaviour for very long. It was easy to tell why I'd been acting so strange. The blood dripped from his original bite wound. His skin is almost dissolving around it, exactly the same as what's happening to specimen fourteen. The moment was bittersweet, because although we could both laugh about it then, it's a reality that we will soon have to face for real. This incident just highlighted that.

CHAPTER 42

ALYSSA

I could jump up and down with excitement. This place looks much better protected than I'd even imagined it would be. Even Pete can't argue with the security this place will provide. I doubt we'd *ever* have to move on from here. I'm sure we could stay here for as long as is necessary—maybe even forever, if that's what it comes down to. Of course, the possibility of that becomes more realistic by the second, but I don't say that to the rest of the group. I can't, especially not after that speech I made. The one that was quite certain we'd all be rescued at some point. Deep down I'm perfectly aware that no one is coming, but I need to act positive, just to keep up morale.

There are a few zombies scattered about the base, all in uniform. They must have been RAF fighters that got left behind in the race to the airport, or they were forced to stay behind due to infection. They look strange, almost comical. They seem much slower and more sluggish than any I've seen before, almost as if any movement is a great effort. Even the sight of us hasn't riled them up *that* much. Of course that could all change when we get within reach, so I won't allow myself to become complacent.

It's decided with barely any communication that Randy, Pete, and I will go inside to clear the area. They both look as quietly confident as I feel. This looks like it's going to be one of the easiest challenges we've had to face. I feel anticipation buzzing through me as we get ready to go in. I grip tightly to the handle of my axe, waiting to start. This time my suggestion to stick together goes down well—luckily everyone is starting to see that my ideas are smart and the right ones to follow. We position ourselves in a circle formation so we can see every angle. This way, we shouldn't have any nasty surprises.

We find a tiny gap in the fence, near to the ground, to climb through. I make a mental note to remember to fix that later. I don't think that the zombies will have the intelligence to think to come through here, but it's far better to be safe than sorry. My heart is pounding as we creep forward; my confidence is beginning to wane. I know we *can* do this, but the reality of the situation is always a little bit terrifying. Plus this time, we have the pressure of everyone watching us. It's a strange sensation, like I have a spotlight shining on me or something—and not just in my imagination this time. I can't re-visualize any mistakes to suit myself. This is much more than me just picturing myself inside some damn movie.

I'm soon distracted by the sound of a blade slashing through rotten skin. It's amazing how quickly you get used to these sounds and can recognise them immediately. I swing around, trying to get myself into the right frame of mind, but Pete has already finished the job without any issues. I feel uneasy as that seemed *far* too easy. I remember how challenging it was to force my blade into Lexi's skull—are the zombies becoming weaker or are we becoming better fighters? I've noticed it more and more as time has passed, when I'm in the middle of a battle, it's all I can focus on.

As much as I want to, I can't delve into my thoughts too deeply right now, because more zombies head towards us. We fight in silence. My axe has absolutely no problems and I can't hear any stress coming from the others. It's only taking single strikes to defeat the zombies in these battles. In previous fights, my aim had to be absolutely perfect and even then it took a few times to *properly* finish them off. I'm pleased by this evolution, but I can't help being confused. I'll have to bring it up with the others later; I need to know their opinions. Especially Emily's. She's clever enough to have a rational answer for me.

I lock eyes with a zombie coming towards me. It's letting out a small, pathetic moan as it slowly shuffles in my direction. It's slow, too slow. It's moving at a snail's pace, making the tension tight. I watch him with fascination, trying to glean some answers about what's going on. In the end I'm forced to break formation, I'm too impatient to wait for it to come to me. I need it gone as quickly as possible.

"Alyssa!" Randy shouts out angrily. I turn, ready to apologise even though as I moved, I felt like my actions were justified. We *did* promise to stick in that position no matter what. But I'm stopped in my tracks by cracked, broken, rotten nails digging down into my shoulder, breaking through my skin.

I freeze, the whole world stops around me. I'm dead, I'm finished, I'm done. I can't believe it. I acted irrationally, stupidly, and it's gotten me killed. A zombie scratch is certain death, everyone knows that. Every single zombie-based film, TV show, and book agrees on that one fact, I'm sure of it. I rack my brain trying to think of an exception, but nothing comes to mind. Even if that is all fiction, it's where so much of my life-saving information has come from, so I can't stop my mind from automatically heading in that direction. My heart beat slows down, almost to a stop. I stare at my axe, wondering what my next move should be. Should I kill myself, or keep fighting until the bitter end? I don't know if it's wise for me to continue on until I turn, then I'll become a danger to the others and one of them will have to kill me. Would it be selfish to give one of my group that responsibility?

They say your life flashes before you when you're about to die. That doesn't happen for me in this moment; just a million thoughts, plans, and ideas rush into my brain at once, so I can't concentrate on a single one of them. I imagine myself trying to grab the words as they float through my mind, trying to understand them, but being frustratingly unsuccessful. Everything going on around me is forgotten. My entire world has become me, by myself, and the large scratch trailing down my back.

I don't know how long I'm stopped still in that state, but suddenly sound bursts back into my ears, making me startle. Pete is pulling me and shouting loudly at me to get a move on. I look down to see the zombie who had his nails in my skin is dead, annihilated on the ground. I don't know who did that, but it was far too late. I'm dead no matter what. I feel like I'm staring at the thing that ended my life for hours, but in reality it's probably only a few seconds.

My eyes snap up and I realise that Pete has pulled me behind a building to hide while he figures out what's happened to me. Randy isn't with us, so he must be still out there, fighting. I slip to the floor, trying to pull myself together. I don't cry, shock is currently consuming me, numbing everything else. Pete shakes me, he's speaking but I can't understand a word he's saying.

Finally his words start to penetrate my brain. "Alyssa, come on! Pull yourself together, is it the scratch? You don't have to worry about that. I've been scratched by the infected in plenty of fights. It doesn't do anything. There's no fluid involved. That's why it *has* to be a bite—didn't you know that? Look." I turn to see scars all over his arms, how have I never noticed them before? "Come on, you've got to get yourself in order, we've still got lots to do. If we want to go inside, we'll need to clear out this building and pretty soon." I stare back in a daze. "Come on, Alyssa." He starts to plead. "Think about the others. We can't leave them outside the fence for too much longer unarmed."

Emily's face fills my mind and gives me the determination and willpower to stand. If what Pete is saying is correct, then I'm actually going to survive, and if that's the case, I need to make sure this place is secure so everyone else can live too. I haven't quite accepted the truth of what's happening yet, but I need to work on that in my own time. Right now I need to get back into battle mode. This is nowhere near over yet.

We walk out to find Randy surrounded by the remaining corpses. He is holding his knees and panting heavily. This battle has been won, at least. Now we need to see how bad the inside is. We need to get it cleared out before it gets dark, unless we want to camp again. I couldn't bear it, especially not being so close to a decent building.

The door to the main building slowly creaks open. I try to get myself to fully focus; I need all my other thoughts to disappear for now. I'm sure I can hear Pete's nervous heart beating from over here. I try to give him a reassuring smile; all the while our fate is being decided.

CHAPTER 43

DR. JONES

April 7th

8:20 a.m.

Ashley.

My Ashley.

Now what do I do? I don't even...

What do I write? She's here. They've brought her in. They've given me my wish, but not in the way I so badly desired. She's no longer my wonderful Ashley. Her beautiful long dark hair is matted with blood. One of her eyes is actually hanging from its socket. Her face is covered in bloody scratches. I can't even bear to look at her. I feel revulsion and shame. That isn't the way you're supposed to feel looking upon your spouse.

I won't consider her a specimen, whatever happens to me now. The smirking bastard that brought her in, deeming her that can just...fuck off. I refuse to play to their shit anymore. This is too far, this is much too far. No one could tolerate this. This is beyond...

Where's Melody? Oh dear God, Melody. I hope they haven't done this to you too. Would they? No. But of course they would. I know that. Deep down, I've now seen enough to know that no one is safe, not even an innocent five-year-old girl. I can't cry anymore.

Ashley's leg is broken, bone is sticking out. Her arm has been dislocated, this isn't from being infected. They've done this to her. What if she knew it was happening? I can't even think. The worst thing of all is her underwear. It has been removed. Why have her knickers been taken off, leaving her with absolutely no dignity? It's clear that she's *suffered extensive wounds to her…to her…*

What have they done to you? I can't even think. I've been violently sick so many times. I'm sweaty and I've pulled out clumps of my hair. I think my face is wet with tears but I don't even know anymore. Am I in a nightmare? I wish I was so none of this would be real. Maybe I've finally lost it. I'd like to think so, but my eyes aren't deceiving me. This hell has become worse than I ever thought possible. There was a split second when I thought I saw recognition in her eyes. She almost looked human. But it was over so quickly that I must have imagined it. That just cannot be possible. Once the victim is that far into infection, there isn't any humanity left. Not that I've seen, anyway…

Ashley. This is all my fault. You've been through God knows what, and it's entirely because of my decisions, because I agreed to do this. This disease is too difficult. I didn't know what I was getting myself in for.

God damn it, Ashley, I've failed you far too many times, but this is beyond anything

I ever thought possible. No man ever imagines their marriage ending up in this condition.

Melody. I really, so very desperately want to think that they wouldn't subject a young child to anything terrible, but these people are evil. They're fucked up. In fact, they need to die. If the world is ruled by them...

It doesn't bear thinking about.

Oh Ashley, what am I going to do? I just—

2:15 p.m.

I've smashed everything up. This whole room. I actually feel sorry because I can't control myself. Jason stopped me before I ended up releasing all of the specimens in my fury. That would have caused chaos. I would have hurt myself and everyone around me. Although does that even matter anymore? I don't know, my brain is all over the place.

I just don't have any idea how to deal with all the rage bubbling up inside me. I'm sad, I'm overwhelmingly upset. I've lost my whole world and I don't know where my beautiful daughter is. I don't know...

I can't—

Ashley, I'll avenge you. You can at least be sure of that. I'll make every fucker that hurt you pay. Mark my words.

6:30 p.m.

My worst fears have been confirmed. I examined Ashley closer. It took everything within me to do so. I was looking at my copy of our wedding photo and I knew I just had to discover the truth. It isn't right for her suffering to be kept a secret.

It wasn't easy, she is well into the third stage of infection, but this is my wife. I confirmed everything I thought I knew. She's been abused, violated. I can't even write down the true extent of what they've done to her, it's too difficult. This is the love of my life, for fuck's sake! I thought she was being looked after, I thought—

I'm going to get them back. I will.

1:35 a.m.

I can't sleep. I doubt I'll ever sleep again.

I've been sitting talking to Ashley—well, what's left of her. I still can't look too closely at her. Her eyes convey all of those sick bastards doing things to her. I can see it, and it cuts me up badly. I've been keeping Jason awake but he hasn't complained once. I think my state of mind is clear.

I know why this has happened. Well, there's no excuse for what they've done to her beforehand. I've been trying my absolute best. But her arrival down here has come at a very convenient time. Yesterday evening, I presented the newest research. Specimen fourteen eventually died of her own accord. It wasn't pretty. It wasn't simple, in fact it was a nightmare, but it happened. Then specimen seventeen quickly followed, proving my theory right. Victims of AM13 deteriorate with nothing to keep them going, until they can no longer carry on. Then they just slowly die. Their bodies just give up. It makes so much sense; it just isn't a quick process.

All we have to do is wait.

Who knows how long Ashley has been infected. Who knows? But they waited until my answer was unsatisfactory before bringing her down here to show me what they're capable of.

I've got to kill them before they do anything to Melody. If they haven't already, of course. They have to die for this. I owe it to everyone. No one can survive this regime, someone needs to put a stop to it, and that person has to be me. I need to make things right. I can't do it for myself, everything has already been stripped away from me, but if Melody is alive, I need to make this world a better place for her. She deserves a chance. All the remaining survivors do. None of them have earned the life they currently have, and will continue to have if no one does anything. This messed up government needs to come to a rapid end before they ruin civilisation irreparably.

The disgusting bastards! I can't wait to

give them what they deserve.

CHAPTER 44

ALYSSA

I rush over to the hole in the fence and beckon the others to come through quickly. I can sense the relief emanating off of them immediately. I never considered how truly worrying it must have been for them during the time we were inside. We were a long time, and they had no idea what was going on. We had to be thorough though, and luckily for us the entire building was empty. That didn't stop us from being extra careful. One room missed could have ended someone's life.

"Go inside," I pant. "It's all completely empty. I'm just going to fill in this hole; I'll see you in there." Emily pauses to wait with me, but I impatiently motion for her to leave. I want to do this by myself, there's something extra I need to do whilst I'm here, and knowing Emily's temperament, I never know how she's going to react to things.

I find some planks of wood which I intend to use, but before that I look around for something to write with. One of the zombie's corpses has a thick black pen in its pocket, which I grab hold of gratefully—it's nice on the odd occasion that things *actually* go my way. I scrawl my message across the wood, pleased at finally doing something positive. I should have thought of this sooner—I would have probably had more luck with it at the church—but at least I'm doing it now.

E. I found your letter at the airport. I've been looking for you ever since. I'm in here. It's safe at this base. Please come in, I'm desperate to find you. A.

I'm pleased with my handiwork. I had to write it quite small, to fit in all I wanted to say, but I'm sure it'll be intriguing enough to bring forward anyone who isn't infected. I consider writing a note to any other survivors to come in too, but decide against it. I don't have any more room and I'm sure that's implied. If I saw it, I wouldn't hesitate to contact whoever's inside. Especially if I was alone.

I don't worry too much as I badly nail the boards up. The zombies are clearly stupid, and I fully intend to check the area every single day for any replies, or people waiting. I'm so eager to find E, I'm so desperate to know who it is. I want to thank them. I don't know where I'd be without all of E's messages. They may not have led me to where they were supposed to, but they did help me find my group. They gave me a reason to carry on.

I rush inside to be met with the loud noise of happy chatter and laughter. Everyone is elated, almost hysterical with our change of fate. For now at least, we're safe. Right at this moment, everyone can rejoice and celebrate. I smile at the boys. They're rushing around playing some games, colour finally returning to their cheeks. This is how it's meant to be. This is how I wanted to live out my zombie apocalypse experience. I thought I wanted it to be all fighting, action, playing the heroine, but now I can see I just need some calm. There needs to be a mix, and as long as I'm with others, the calm part can be just as fun as the action. The relaxing sensation that I've taken for granted so many times is all I've ever really desired.

I almost skip over to Emily and throw my arm around her shoulders, grinning wildly at her. Suddenly, it feels like everyone turns to stare at us, so I quickly let my arm drop. My heart is racing, her skin felt electric on mine and I realise that I really need to start being careful. This is all going to end in tears and I can't bear the thought of hurting anyone.

* * *

The days begin to pass in a blur of activity. We all rub along nicely and I've even begun to relax a lot more around Emily. I was just being silly, all the heightened emotions were due to the surrounding situation, and it was unfair of me to put any of that on her. We all have jobs and activities to get us through the days. One of mine is checking the fence every day for E. So far, no luck. I haven't given up hope, though. I'll find out who E is, even if I eventually have to go out looking. I can sense that this intriguing question will be answered one way or another, so I'm not too impatient.

This place was fully stocked with everything we could possibly need. It even has a generator, but we're saving that for when it's really necessary. For when it gets unbearably cold and very dark. Everyone is brighter, lighter, and happier here. The danger feels a thousand miles away. The odd zombie crashes against the fence, but a simple knife to the head through the bars is so easy. I could almost let myself believe that they're decreasing in numbers, but I don't want to get too excited, we have no idea what's going on in the built up areas. Cities could still be absolutely full of zombies.

The boys have the best of both worlds. The safety of indoors, with the ability to play outside. Albeit quietly and supervised, but it's the best they could hope for in this situation. It's the closest thing to a normal life we could ever experience in the zombie apocalypse. I actually prefer this life to the one I had before, pre-zombies. I'm starting to find myself, to work out who I really am. I feel like I matter, like I'm finally becoming a 'real' person. I feel settled inside myself. It's amazing how much of my life was spent confused, a turbulent mess, and I didn't even notice it. I still wish I hadn't lost my family, but in a way, this is the best thing that could have happened to me.

I've confided in Emily how much easier the zombies have become to kill, just as I planned to. She has many theories, of course, which she has tried to confirm whilst Randy, myself, or Pete kill one through the fence. She agrees that they seem to be regressing, falling apart. She thinks that the virus is actually consuming them from the inside out, and soon they'll completely succumb to it and die out all by themselves. The human body can only take so much damage before it'll simply give up. Even though that goes against every single thing I know about zombies, I can't help but feel that she's right. It *does* comply with everything I've seen. I guess I just need to accept that Hollywood doesn't always get it right.

The most important thing that I can take from this is that we're going to be the survivors of AM13. It's looking like we're going to outlive it. Maybe not getting on the plane was the best thing to happen to me. The people that left the UK could all be dead; we could be all that's left. And if they do come back, I'm sure they'll be shocked at how well we've done stuck here with nothing.

Everything is just fantastic.

CHAPTER 45

ETHAN

I keep having this odd feeling, like I'm being watched. Like someone is out there, looking for me. Of course, this is just my mind playing games with me, because there *is* no one left! I know that for a fact. If there *was* anyone watching me, they would be infected. In that case, I would be dead already.

I refuse to die here though, out on the streets. That's not how I'm going to go. I've made my plan, and that's *exactly* how it's going to work out, I'm certain of it. There is no other solution for me. I can only go when I've found her.

Leah.

Leah.

Leah.

I say her name with every step I take, like it's my new tick. She's my motivation, my goal. She's all I need to keep me going. Without that target, I have nothing.

By the time I actually get to Leah, I'm going to

be glad of her tearing me apart and killing me—I'll be begging for it! As long as my plan comes to fruition just as I want it to, I'll be happy to die. I can't stand another second in this disease-ridden hell.

Earth is no more. The planet belongs to *them* now. It's either die or join them. That's the only options left, and I can't stand the thought of becoming one of those shuffling, cannibalistic monsters. I wouldn't be able to cope. Even now, the thought of AM13 coursing through me fills me with an unbridled panic. That's why my plan is so perfect. Leah has been deprived of a food source for such a long time that she'll devour me in seconds. It'll be over before I even know it.

My only problem is it's taking me forever to get back to my home—to her. I can only move in short bursts because my energy levels are so low. My body has no fuel whatsoever, so it keeps giving up on me. It's not even like I can keep on going until I can't anymore, before resting, I always have to have *some* energy in the reserves for when I need to fight. I cannot allow myself to be left with no chance of fighting. That'll ruin everything I've been working so hard to achieve.

I don't think I'm far though—not anymore. I might even be able to make it within the next 48 hours. A couple more days and I'll be gone. Not another thought or worry to concern me ever again. Even my booming doomsday voice will be no more. This will be the one thing that silences it forever.

I'm just going to wait here for a little while, just to recover. All I need is a *little* bit more strength before I get up and go again. Then it won't be long.

Just for a few more moments…

CHAPTER 46

DR. JONES

April 8th

5:15 a.m.

I can't even cope with all of the violent thoughts swirling around in my head anymore. It's wearing me out, tearing me down.

How am I supposed to sit there and see my wife going through all of this, knowing that her last uninfected hours were full of torture and abuse? I've never thrown up so many times; horrific images just keep spinning through my mind, however much I try to stop them. I can just see everything they've done to her. I wish I had some brandy or something. Some alcohol to numb the pain. I've never been a drinker, but now feels like as good a time as any to hit the bottle.

I keep trying to kill Ashley, to put her out of her misery, but I'm too scared—still too in love with her. I can't do it. I need to, I should do. It's how any decent man would act, but I'm too afraid. As much as I know that there's nothing left, I can't let her go. I'm letting my wife down yet again.

There's no cure, no antidote for AM13. If someone created this disease, then well-fucking-done. What an amazing job you've done, you wanker. My mission was futile from the start. I had no chance; I was battling against something that's indestructible, except by natural causes. If only the board had seen that, rather than punishing me for being unable to do the impossible.

I keep thinking it through over and over and I don't know if Ashley would even want to 'be cured' from this after what she's been *through, and I don't just mean the extensive damage to her body. I mean with the memories of all of the shit they've put her through. Oh God, my poor Ashley, who never did anything bad to anyone. She's been through things that no woman, no human deserves. How can people be so disgusting? How can people do such things? I've never ever understood evil.*

I keep trying to think back over our happier times, but each memory is tainted with this version of my wife. It's as if I can't even remember what she was like before. They've ruined everything. Everything. They've stripped me of my whole life, and for what? It hasn't done any good. I can't solve the unsolvable, whatever they do to me. I'm sure they have more up their sleeves but it doesn't change a damn thing.

The fucking horrible bastards.

They've belittled, controlled, brutalised and demoralised the people who've managed to survive the horrors of AM13 and the Lockdown failure. Hasn't the human race been through enough? Apparently I haven't. It seems they think I deserved to see my beloved in this condition. How? Why? This isn't right. It isn't. No.

I'm done. This is over now. They're going to pay. In fact, I'm going to kill them all, slowly and painfully. For myself, for Ashley, for Melody, for everyone that's left alive. We don't need to be ruled by these men. After all the horrid things we've been through, things don't want to be rebuilt under the rulings of psychopaths. No, we need a civilised way to rebuild. It needs to be done with kind hands, not this fucking crap that they seem to think is the way forward. It's very simple. They need to die.

I'm going to fucking kill every single one of them!

Read this promise now. Every single one of them will die by my hands.

8:45 p.m.

I've told Jason what I'm going to do. He told me to sleep on the idea before acting irrationally. I respect him; I always have, so I agreed. He may be right. I've never been like this before, maybe there is a better way? Do they deserve better? Do I? I'll have to live with what I've done. Or will I? I lay on my bed all day, unable to sleep. However, I think I've managed to calm down. Bursts of rage keep making their appearance, but my thoughts are much more rational and controlled. This time I know my thoughts are correct.

Do you know what? I'm still going to do it. Nothing will stop me. I know what's right and wrong. Rape, murder, torture and forcing infection on someone deserves death. I'm sure there is no one who would disagree with that conclusion. Even if I am biased because of my family's involvement, I still think I would be considered to be doing the right thing.

On hearing my decision, Jason decided it was time to tell me more tales of the mistreatment he knows about, happening in the campsite outside. It seems rape is actually a very common factor, murder is normal, and he heard many rumours of the people in charge keeping infected in cages outside on the outskirts of the campsite, as a warning, as a permanent threat. He took little notice at the time, but now after everything he's seen, he thinks it makes total sense. It's how the random flare-ups of AM13 keep developing, and it isn't exactly as if the board members are rational thinking, decent human beings. In fact, now he's sure that many of the people that have been infected have been so on purpose as punishment or their children have suffered AM13 in their place.

That tells me why I've been able to obtain so many specimens. It also explains how new people have been becoming infected in this supposed 'safe haven.' Everything about it is starting to come together. The psychopaths have been using this virus as a weapon. That's so messed up, it's ludicrous, ridiculous. It's just unbelievable.

I can't stop thinking about Melody, my

little angel. I'm convinced that she's infected as much as my poor heart wants to be wrong. She's probably being kept in a cage, being used to infect others. I don't know if it's true, but my instincts tell me that nothing good has happened. I guess I've lost all hope.

With Jason on my side, we're both going to kill them all. I finally feel happy again. No, not happy. I'll never be happy again. I feel empowered. I know I'm going to win this battle, I'm going to help.

I'll be useful.

I'm going to make these murders my best work yet. Fuck everything else I've tried to achieve. This is it. My crowning glory. The one thing that I'm remembered for. My job that changes everything for the better. I'm going to save the world.

Fuck you, so called ~~board members~~. I will win this. I'll win and you will die!

I'm doing this for myself, but also for everyone else. Does that make this mission noble or just a revenge fantasy? Who cares, by this point I'm probably insane. At least, I wish I was. I wouldn't feel so deeply.

CHAPTER 47

ALYSSA

Until it isn't.

Things are no longer fantastic. In fact, they're awful; I can't even begin to describe how bad it's all become.

Randy is dead. Dead. He's died and I no longer have any idea what to do with myself. I can't actually believe it. I can't even say the words out loud. Randy, the glue that held this group together, is just…gone. At first I thought he'd been bitten, that maybe one of the zombies had gotten him through the fence. I panicked that somehow one of them had made their way inside. But I was wrong, very wrong.

Only days before, Randy had finally confided in Sarah that he'd been suffering with a rare heart condition for a very long time, and that he was beginning to struggle without his medication. I want to scream, to cry out. Why didn't he mention it during the time we were out on supply runs, we could have picked up the tablets for him. Of course we would have, gathering medication was *his* idea. But it's too late now. What difference is saying all of that going to bring to this circumstance? Nothing. It's gone too far, the damage is already done.

Why didn't I notice him becoming ill? Has my obsession with looking out for E made me unable to see anything else? Was I so determined to believe that everything was amazing, that my brain didn't allow me to witness a terrible event occurring? I thought I'd gotten past the stage of deluding myself. Obviously I'm not as grown up as I want to be.

Leon is inconsolable—we all are, of course—but it's hit him particularly hard. I'm sure he lost his mother to the zombies earlier on in the apocalypse. No one has ever said it, but I could sense it when I first joined the group. I was always going to ask, but never got around to it. Now I'll never know and even worse, Leon has been left alone. What a wasted life. After all that Randy's survived, all that we've been through together, and now he's been taken by another illness entirely. One that I'm sure we could have helped manage if only we'd known about it.

I've been sitting on my bed in silence, staring at the same spot on the wall ever since I found out about it this morning. Sarah found his corpse, and woke us all up in a screaming panic. She's still hysterical. I don't think anyone can calm her down, I'm unsure if she'll ever recover, to be honest. All of us are going to be so badly affected by the loss of Randy; he was so integral to our survival.

The tears finally begin cascading down my

cheeks, the numbness finally giving into emotion. Suddenly I feel a pair of soft arms slowly making their way around my neck. Emily. She always seems to arrive at exactly the right moment. I nestle into her, leaning all of my body against her, soaking up her body heat. I try to speak through the sobs, but my words are stilted and jumbled. I'm trying to convey that I can't go on anymore, that I want to stop this nightmare. That everything has become too much for me. Any confidence I ever had in myself was always misplaced. I used it to mask the pain. Now I can't hold it in anymore. I'm done.

Before I even realise it, before I can even think, her lips are crashing down on mine. I respond enthusiastically, ferociously kissing Emily back. I'm caught up in grief and I'm enjoying the feeling of giving myself entirely to someone. Her hands have become tangled up in my hair and I'm holding onto her cheek tenderly. This moment feels so right. Any weirdness I may have thought I was feeling was incorrect. I had my mind all mixed up, I wasn't frightened about giving her the wrong impression, I *wanted* her. I didn't want to push her away; I wanted to pull her in close. I want her so badly I could explode. Her soft lips feel amazing against mine, they fit perfectly. Her delicate tongue slips into my mouth and fireworks and butterflies burst in my stomach. I fall into her; I let this moment whisk me away. I melt, my heart falling in love.

Soon my brain kicks back into action, and I roughly shove Emily off me. I run off mumbling a pathetic apology as I do. Now I'm desperate to be alone, I need to get myself in order. I rush into one of the bathrooms, locking the door behind me. My body slumps to the floor as the weeping starts up again. I'm now crying for Randy, for Emily, and for myself. What have I done? Why did I let myself get carried away by the moment? My *one* rule was not to get involved with anyone during the zombie apocalypse, not to get too close. I didn't want to hurt anyone, especially not Emily. I love her, I do. But I can't love her in that way, can I? I'm not even a lesbian. I can't remember a time I've ever been attracted to a girl before. What is going on?

I try to calm my mind. I need to think straight, I want to give myself a rational reason for the events that transpired, but I can't. When we were kissing, I felt complete. I felt like the missing piece of my puzzle came together. I've never experienced feelings so powerful before, I've never been so attracted to anyone in my life. My heart is still racing with the adrenaline.

Is it real, or is it circumstantial? How do I figure that out? It really doesn't matter either way, I can't let it continue. I have to stop it before it becomes an issue.

I stay sitting on the cold tiled floor until a soft knock wakes me up from my stupor. I stand, shaking, wondering if it's going to be Emily confronting me right away. I try to plan what I'm going to say but my thoughts are still scattered. It's Sarah, she has organised a funeral for Randy. It won't be anything over the top, just a simple way for us to say goodbye. She thinks it'll be good for us all to pay our respects to such a wonderful man, and to remember how sacred death really is. It's so easy to forget that in the zombie apocalypse.

As we say our final goodbyes, burying a great man, I don't make eye contact with anyone. I feel even worse as I listen to everyone speak. How could I hurt Emily now, in such a terrible way? My whole face is soaking with tears. Randy was wonderful, he wasn't the shambolic mess that I am. He deserved to live far more than I do. That's the first time I've felt that way about someone, and all of a sudden I feel that way about absolutely everyone. I shouldn't have survived this long; it isn't fair on anyone else. I'm the one that should be in that shallow grave. A hollow hopelessness that I've experienced only once before consumes me all over again.

As soon as it's over, I rush off and climb into bed. If I shut my eyes I know no one will bother me. I don't want to talk, I don't want to think. I just want to be by myself with a blank mind. I need to shut the rest of the world out.

CHAPTER 48

DR. JONES

April 12th

9:45 a.m.

This is it. It's time to act. The hour is upon us.

Jason is a genius. An evil genius that I'm so glad is on my side. He's more brilliant than I ever gave him credit for. His mind is sick, twisted, almost gory. It's exactly what I need to spur me on. He's driving me forward, making this much easier to go through. Without him, I might have given up on my idea, I may have lost enthusiasm, but with the constant visual reminder of my poor Ashley, and Jason's words, I'm ready. I know what I need to do and I will make it happen.

Jason was never like this in stage one, I wonder if it's the AM13 virus raging inside him, desperate to spread itself that's turned him into this messed up, sadistic bastard. To be honest, I don't give a fuck why he's like this, what is causing it. It's absolutely perfect. I need him to be this way. We need each other to get this done.

I can barely stand to look at my wife anymore, it's terrible. Ashley is in such a terrible way, it's making me so sick. I have to keep watching her, to spur me forward, but I won't pretend it isn't the toughest thing that I've ever, ever done. She's banging her detached arm against the door over and over. I've tried begging her to stop, pleading with her to remember me, showing her photographs, telling her about our life. Of course this does nothing. That part of her brain is gone. She no longer has any memories, I'm nothing to her. Now she just sees me as something to infect, or something to eat. I don't recall what conclusion I reached in the end. None of it matters anyway; it makes no difference to the outcome of the victims. Nothing does. This virus, it's a powerful one.

Jason came up with a brilliant plan. It's fucking amazing! It'll ensure that the bastards who did this to Ashley will suffer. Their deaths will be slow and painful, and they'll get to experience what they have done to everyone else. I can't wait to administer it upon them.

Jason will be in stage three soon—deep into it. This fact is inevitable. He's already showing signs of waning, but as with the rest of his descent into AM13, it seems to be going slowly, allowing him to maintain some humanity. As much as my heart bleeds over his loss, it's essential to the plan. It's a shame that such a wonderful man has to be sacrificed, but it's difficult to see it in that way when he will die anyway. Maybe he is more of a martyr? Who really knows, his death will ultimately be highly significant in ridding the world of this evil.

He's going to tell me when it's time. That point is pivotal. When he's almost at the point of really losing himself, then we begin. Then I'm going to release him and Kevin Hall and 'John Smith'—I desperately wish that I knew his name. It's such a shame for an unnamed person to aid in the saving of all of these people, but I really have no information to go from...

When Jason's ready, I'll send them into the boardroom and let havoc ensue. They will tear the people in charge, the ones who have made all these shitty decisions, to shreds, infecting them as they go. Doing unto them as they have done unto everyone else. Giving them exactly what they deserve. However much could go wrong, this much will go right. These fuckers will get exactly what's coming to them.

It means I'll lose Jason, of course, but unfortunately that's happening anyway. It's sad to see his descent, it's heart-wrenching, just as I knew it would be, but he's quite upbeat and positive about it all now he knows he's going to put his infected self to good use. He's happy to help save the world. So am I, even if it isn't in the way I originally had planned. But I suppose, in many ways, this is much, much better.

Of course I could die too, but I have nothing left to live for anyway, so I really don't care. With no remaining family and a career in tatters, what's left for me? What sort of life will I be able to lead post AM13—if there is a post AM13, of course. That all depends on how accurate my research really is! If I do manage to survive, I'll do what I need to and put Ashley down. It's a terrifying, horrifying thought, but I just know it's what needs to be done.

Then, if I make it that far, I'll go out and find Melody, do the same to her. My poor, beautiful little princess. I so want to believe that you're alive, but my subconscious knows you're gone. I can just feel that your wonderful spirit is no longer on this disgusting planet. You're somewhere much more deserving of you. But your body needs to be let go too. I'll be brave. I will do it. I'll be the man, the husband, the father that I'm supposed to be. The man that I should have been during the whole time I was neglecting my responsibilities, putting more time and effort into my pointless job than my loving family. I can't take back my decisions, but abandoning them after the Lockdown was the most God damn stupid thing I've ever done. Ever.

God, how I want to string all the boardroom fuckers up, cut them piece by piece. Make them watch as I remove their genitals, the disgusting members that defiled my wife. I would make them eat their own body parts, laugh as they're violently sick. I would dislocate their limbs, as they've clearly done to others. Infect them with the vicious AM13 virus and pierce bullet holes into their bodies. Make them suffer a taste of their own medicine. Then I could parade them around as they deteriorate into a black, sludgy nothing. I'd enjoy everyone's cheers as they see that I've saved them. As they witness what I've done to them to avenge what they've had done to others. It would be a great moment. I'd be hailed a hero; everyone would know I'd made them safe from the psychopathic dictators that have been driven mad by false power.

Well, soon they won't be able to do that anymore. The pigs. The fucking disgusting twats. I hate them. There are no God damn words to describe how much I hate them.

I can't do that of course. I fantasise over it repeatedly, but following through would be a whole different matter. I'm sure I would be caught by the soldiers as I act anyway, and overpowering all of the board members would provide another obstacle that would be challenging to overcome.

No. None of that matters, as fun as it would be. What we have is so much better.

I wish I could find all of the family members of these specimens, tell them exactly what they did, let them know that they helped save everyone. Make them proud. But of course I can't. I won't live that long. What use am I without my family? I'm nothing without them. I'll be so glad to make it even that far, but I'm quite sure that I won't. Really, this is my last hurrah!

Unless I find Melody. That will change everything.

As much as it would be poetic justice, I'll keep Ashley here. I can't put my beautiful wife through anymore. I won't make her face her attackers again. Once the others have gone to carry out the deed, I will put her down. I may have been bitten by this point, but I can still do this. I can't even begin to guarantee that the specimens won't get to me. I'll try of course, I'll hide and Jason is going to move loudly, to keep the attention of the others on him, but who knows how foolproof that plan is. In fact, it isn't foolproof at all. But it's still amazing. It's still the best damn thing to happen since I've been locked up in this nightmare. It's still the best way I'm going to get revenge and we're going to help all the civilians stuck *here. It's necessary and perfect for what needs to be done.*

We've examined it from every single angle, we've worked out every single thing that could go wrong—and believe me, there's a whole lot—but the end result will be effective. Even if all the board members aren't killed, I'm pretty sure they'll be running scared. It'll show them that they aren't invincible; it'll let them know that someone is after them, coming for them. Even if I'm dead, it leads the way for others to take over the attack. It sends a message. We won't take the bullshit 'rules' from nobodies lying down. The power of the many, of the people, is more powerful than them. AM13 has ripped up civilisation, it's changed all of our lives for the worst. There has been so much that we haven't been able to control, but who rebuilds our lives is in our hands. This is the time to establish what we want. I'm certain that I'm not the only one who can see this.

Revenge is going to be a dish served ice

cold. I wish I could be around long enough to watch the life leave all of their revolting eyes, but doing my piece is enough. I'm going to be important in this; even in my death my name will be remembered. I've done so much; I've actually achieved quite a lot. It's taking my impending doom for me to see it. My entire existence hasn't been wasted, but this is it. This is what it's all been building up for. This, right here, is my life's purpose.

CHAPTER 49

ALYSSA

The moment comes way before I'm ready for it.

"Still avoiding me, huh?" I glance up to see Emily's bright blue eyes gazing back at me, fully of unanswered questions and hurt.

"I…I um, I don't…"I stutter, trying to find a way to dispute her claims, but I can't. We both know that she's right. A blush fills my cheeks as I try to find a way to convey the truth. How do I tell her that I'm afraid? That these emotions are too much? I can't face dealing with them. I don't know how to admit that Emily blurs all of my vision. I'm in complete and utter awe of her. She's an obsession that I cannot shake. But I can't act on my feelings, even if I wanted to. Now just isn't the time.

Emily lets out a deep sigh; her whole body seems to deflate with it. "Look, I shouldn't have kissed you." The words come out stiffly, as if they're tricky to say. "It was wrong, I know that now. I don't want it to affect the group, so can we just forget it?" She doesn't look at me, even once, so I can't gauge any of her emotions. I don't know if this is what she really wants, I sense that deep down, there's a whole lot more she wants to say.

So I nod feebly, knowing this is really the time that I need to speak out and make everything all right again, but my tongue is tied and my throat is dry like sandpaper. I watch her sadly as she turns abruptly and stalks away, wishing dreadfully that I wasn't a wimp. Wishing that I could do something, anything to turn this whole thing around.

Suddenly my heart starts pounding heavily and my brain goes fuzzy with emotion. My legs start moving before I can stop them, before I can even consider what it is my body's doing. A hollow feeling in my stomach tells me that if I don't do this now, then I never will. I'll lose Emily forever. That feeling alone is more terrifying than accepting emotions that I don't understand. It's more frightening than any zombie I've ever faced, any horror I've endured. I've never felt a fear like it.

I grab her shoulder and roughly pull her towards me. I push my lips onto hers, no longer caring about any of my previous 'rules' or decisions. This feels right, which means it must *be* right. Yes, we could die tomorrow, so shouldn't we embrace life now? Of course it'll hurt if I lose Emily, but at least I'll have the knowledge that I followed my heart and had something amazing, for however long it lasts. I won't have regret, and that's something.

A warm sensation erupts and encloses around us, the rest of the world melts away. An involuntary moan escapes my throat as the kiss deepens. My heart almost bursts from my chest; I never ever want this feeling or this moment to end. This is perfect. It's amazing.

We break apart, panting for breath and I let out a nervous laugh. I wish I could convey my apology with my eyes. I try to communicate that I was acting crazy and it won't happen again. I don't know if the message is received, but Emily finally looks happy. She looks relaxed. In this moment, all of her previous strange moods become clear. They were all my fault, my constant rejections burned her deeply. I didn't even realise I was doing it. I lean forward again, pursing my lips. I don't know how to *say* what I mean, I don't have the right words within me, but I can show Emily how much she means to me. I can make up for my mistakes with actions.

* * *

The next morning, I awaken with a huge grin on my face. Last night was simply amazing, it was monumental. Emily is so beautiful; having her body tangled with mine all through the night was remarkable. I'll never be able to experience anything so wonderful again. I look down at her blonde hair sweeping across my chest and sigh with contentment. I'm in love. I'm one hundred percent, definitely in love. Or at least lust. Either way, it feels exhilarating.

My bladder forces me to move way before I want to. I tiptoe quietly out of the room, pulling on an oversized man's t-shirt that was left behind here as I go. As I wander down the halls, I try to keep my face straight. I want to look innocent. I don't want anyone to know what happened between me and Emily. I want it to be our little secret, at least for now. Constant scrutiny always ruins things, especially as one of the people who is bound to show a lot of interest is Sarah, Emily's mum.

I bump into Pete as I emerge from the bathroom. He looks strange; green, sweaty, and panicky. I grab hold of him as he almost falls to the ground. He tries to talk to me for a while, but his words are garbled and make no sense. I force him to drink cool water until he's calmed down enough to tell me what's going on. The worry never leaves his expression, the whole time he speaks.

"I need to get out of here, Alyssa. I need to go on a supply run or something. I can't just stay here where Randy died. I need a break from this place. Just a few hours. Anything." I'm absolutely stunned. I had no idea that Randy's death had affected Pete so badly. I didn't know he cared enough about any of us to feel this way. His grief is making him act crazy. "I can't just…sit and—"

"Okay, okay, Pete," I interrupt quickly. "I'll go with you. I'll come out with you when you decide to leave." I know this mission is unnecessary and dangerous, but sometimes you just have to do something, however little it makes sense. I understand his irrational need; sometimes this apocalyptic life feels claustrophobic. I'm not about to let Pete do something stupid by himself while he's vulnerable. "I'll do it, Pete, but the earliest we can go is tomorrow, not today. You aren't well; you're not yourself at the moment. So tomorrow, if you still want to go, we will. Okay? You need to calm yourself down first, get yourself back on track."

He nods, grateful that I didn't immediately shoot his insane idea down. He goes off to his bed, reassuring me that he will sleep, and I watch him leave, deeply worried about his state of mind. I didn't tell Pete the whole truth. I also don't want to leave until tomorrow because I'm not quite ready to be separated from Emily yet. I want to cling to this happiness for a little while longer before I'm forced onto a fool's errand.

Emily is awake when I walk back into my room. She has the sheets draped around her and her bed head makes her look sexier than ever. I take in a deep breath before telling her about the exchange I just had with Pete. She riles up with immediate fury and I kiss her hard to stop her rant before it can even begin.

"Em, I doubt it'll even happen. Tomorrow Pete will have forgotten all about it. Just don't worry about it, okay?" She looks doubtful, but thankfully lets the subject drop.

I knew Emily wouldn't understand Pete's need to get out as much as I do. We're cut from the same cloth. Me and Pete silently just 'get' each other. Instead of trying to explain, I spend the rest of the day ensuring that we continue the wonderful time that we've been having, now our feelings are out in the open. Of course, we make a separate appearance to meals and for our chores, neither of us ready to go public with our newly found relationship, but every spare moment we find is spent together, alone.

When the night rolls around, we cuddle up in my bed again. Emily's arms are wrapped around my neck and her nose is touching mine, so we are breathing in each other's breath. I'm just staring at her beautiful features as she sleeps soundly, trying to live in the moment. But I can't stop my mind worrying about what the next day will hold. Despite my reassurances, I know Pete will still want to go and I'm just a bit worried. Now I have someone to live for, the pressure to survive is so much higher. It's everything I feared it would be. It's exactly why I attempted to avoid anything like this happening, although now it has, I don't regret it at all.

I push my lips softly down onto Emily's, being careful not to wake her, as I say a silent goodbye.

Just in case.

CHAPTER 50

DR. JONES

April 18th

9:25 a.m.

This is it. The end. It's arrived at last. The moment is here. Everything is over. Finally this nightmare is done. It's time for the plan to begin. The moment I've been waiting for. I feel...I don't know how I feel, really. The anticipation is heightening all of my senses. I guess I just feel weird. I suppose that's the only word for it.

Weird. Strange. Odd. Bizarre. Peculiar. Unusual.

I've been pacing around the room for the last hour or so, looking at all of my equipment and do you know what? I'm going to miss it. Can you fucking believe how crazy I've become?! I'm in the middle of the fucking war to end everything, and I'm getting sentimental over a few fucking test tubes. I've lost my freaking mind. This room has been nothing but awful for me. It's been my own personal torture chamber; it's where all of my worst nightmares have come true. It's hell, full of demons, and I feel a weird sadness at leaving it behind.

I don't even know what's going on anymore. I can't even remember who I am. Is that weird or what? Fuck it, it doesn't matter anymore. I don't matter anymore. None of us do. This isn't about us anymore; it's about making things better for others.

Jason is nearing his demise. The inevitable is happening. I'm too concerned with the plan now to be as sad as I should be. He looks a complete and utter God damn mess, to be honest. I've never seen him look so bloody awful. AM13 doesn't suit him at all. At all. I think he's more excited than me about the oncoming onslaught. He's bloodthirsty, I can see it. It's terrifying and compelling all at the same time. I would look at him scientifically, but I really don't care anymore. He wants to kill and maim and I want the same from him. That's all that matters anymore.

I look at him and laugh. I don't know why I do that because inside I'm silently crying. I mean, how am I really supposed to feel?! I'm upset because I want to feel the human sadness, but I can't. I'm numb and void. I've become solely focused on this plan. This war.

Ashley's dead to me now. I can look at her. I can see her. If I want to, I can touch her, but she's gone. She's dead. She was no longer alive from the second she was brought in here, but I just didn't know how to accept it. I mean, how are you supposed to come to terms with any of this? My wife, my marriage, my life has been stripped away from me. These fucking evil monsters have taken it all! I'm going to make them pay and I'm going to love every God damn second of their pain. They deserve to feel what I have, what we all have.

Maybe I'm bloodthirsty too. I certainly can't wait to see their limbs ripped violently from their bodies. Their screams will fill me with a morbid satisfaction. This has to happen to them. They need this as much as I do. I'm saving every single person whose trapped here under the fucking dictatorship of this psycho bastards.

None of it makes any sense!!! What the fuck did I do to deserve it?

Any of it.

5:35 p.m.

It's time.

It's happening. Jason has just told me that he's ready to go. He's actually finally ready for this to happen. Much as I'd prepared myself, when the moment arrives, I panics lightly. A whole range of unsuspecting emotions run through me, but I push all of that aside. Now isn't the time to start 'feeling' things. I'm just about to get Kevin *and John ready to go. I said thank you to them. I think they understood. They looked at me like they did. But who knows? Maybe I'm imagining things. I'm probably just completely mental now.*

Maybe the whole thing isn't real. Maybe I'm going to wake up in a minute, Ashley next to me, cuddling in to me. Melody in the next room, sound asleep. This whole thing a nightmare.AM13 is some messed up dream. The Lockdown, the laboratory just some mad construct of my imagination.

No, I'm not that lucky. I'm living in this nightmare. It's been thrust upon me. However much I want it to disappear, it isn't going to. I can't keep getting confused between fact and fiction. I don't even know if I am getting confused—that's how messed up my mind is. Everything is fuzzy. Except the plan, that's the only crystal clear thing I can focus on.

This report started out as a scientific research into the AM13 virus, but turned into some Dear Diary shit along the way.

Sorry for that, whoever is reading this. If anyone ever reads this. I hope that someone does, there is some useful stuff in here, I'm sure of it. It tells a lot of truths anyway. If you can sift through all of the crap, I'm sure you'll find something.

I don't really want to be just remembered for what I'm about to do, more for what I've done—the progress towards a cancer cure, the details about the AM13 virus. But they've done unspeakable things to my family. They've probably done unspeakable things to everyone. I hope that's understood, I hope that point gets across, even if nothing else does. I hope people understand why this necessary step had to be taken. I know I'm right, I know this is the right thing to do, even if no one else does understand. Even if I'm viewed as the villain forever.

No, that can't happen. That would be so unfair. Revenge is the only answer. What else would teach them, how else will they learn? No one else is brave enough to do what me and my team of Jason, Kevin, and John are doing. We're the heroes. Maybe this is what I was supposed to do all along, it just took me until now to realise it.

These repetitive thoughts keep going over and over in my mind. Have I written all of them down? Am I repeating myself? Who knows?

The main point is, these fuckers need to die, and this is where it's going to happen. I guess it's time to say 'goodbye cruel world.'

Or maybe a big 'Fuck you' *would work better.*

Everyone gets what they deserve; everything works out the way it's supposed to. Doesn't it?

I can't start considering if I'm right or wrong. It's too late.

Anyway, I am right. I am.

It's time.

It's time.

It's time.

It's time—

CHAPTER 51

ALYSSA

I'm not ready for morning, but it comes along regardless. My heart sinks into my shoes as the enormity of the day hits me. I know Pete will be still ready to go. He *has* to; nothing anyone can say or do will change that. He'll go stir crazy with grief without this, even if it makes no sense to everyone else. He's decided on this mission, and it'll happen one way or another. It's up to me to keep him alive. I'm the only one that can go with him and defend him if he becomes overwhelmed. I don't want to complain. After all, I'm sure he would do the same for me. That's what being in a group is all about, but it doesn't make the challenge any easier to digest. Especially not now, while things are so rough and so amazing all at the same time.

Emily's eyes are wet with tears as she wakes up, as if she's been crying in her sleep. She barely speaks for a while, and I know she's frightened of the emotion overcoming her. I feel the same way, but I need to keep an air of confidence circling me. If she knows that I'm afraid, it'll frighten her so much more.

I don't say the word 'goodbye' aloud even once. I can't, it's layered with too much pressure, and it suggests I may not return. Instead, I use the phrase "We'll see you in a bit" to every single person. I can see the confusion, the worry in all of their faces, and I can't do anything to dispel it. All I need to do is get through this with Pete and get back before nightfall. The sooner we return the better, for everyone's peace of mind. Hopefully Pete will come back much better off and ready to move on. It's hard for all of us, but we need to be strong. Especially for Leon.

We try to leave quietly, without too much of a fuss, but everyone waits at the fence to see us off. I glance back, wishing I could have kissed Emily one last time before leaving, but as no one knows and it's still too soon to tell, I had to just hug her close. All the words I wanted to whisper in her ears had to be left unsaid. If I'd uttered anything to do with love, we could've been overheard and she would've immediately assumed the worst. I just know the way Emily's mind works.

As we jog alongside the road, the RAF base becoming a dot in the distance, I try to make light conversation about the journey that lies ahead of us, but soon realise that it isn't working. This is going to be all the more challenging than any of the previous trips outside that we've had. This one doesn't have a point, a conclusion that we need to reach. This is all about Pete's emotions. I have no idea how long it's going to take for this to be done. Emotion spells trouble, and this is full of it.

Suddenly, I realise that Pete's no longer in my peripheral vision. He isn't running alongside me anymore. I turn back to see him crumpled to the ground in tears. Anxiety grips me. I don't know how to deal with this; I'm no good at confronting my own feelings, never mind the turbulence of others. This situation makes us vulnerable and I can't cope with that at all. This is a terrible place for a breakdown.

I turn back, determined that this needs to be the stopping point of our expedition. I'll comfort him the best I can whilst he's upset, then I'll bring him back to the base, where we're safe and he can feel however he wants. Hopefully this is the thing he needed to do. Hopefully this is him getting it out of his system. If he just wanted to do this away from the prying eyes of everyone else, he's achieved it, so there really is no need to continue on.

I reach down and touch his shoulder, but he violently jerks me off. Unsure of what I need to do for the best, I sit beside him ready to wait it out. I can sense that my silence is needed. I keep vigilant the entire time, every single shadow spelling danger. I can't relax for even a second. I've gotten far too used to the security of the base; it's been so long since I've been out here in the cruel world. Being outside no longer suits me at all. I can fight, of course, but it's been such a long time now, will the skill still be there? Do I still have the quick reflexes that I always relied on?

"Pete I—" As I turn to face Pete again, I'm

stunned by his lips roughly connecting with mine. It feels strange; familiar but alien all at the same time. I quickly realise that I don't like it. I push him off as swiftly as my brain starts working again, knowing that I'm going to hurt his feelings, but also sure that kissing is the wrong thing for us to be doing. Pete isn't the one I want to be this close to. He never has been.

"No, I don't—we need to get going…"I trail off feebly. I'm trying to be considerate with my words, but his mood predictably turns to anger anyway. His eyes darken and he frowns intently, furrowing his eyebrows.

"Why the hell not, Alyssa? What's wrong with me? I could be the last guy on Earth and you still aren't interested. How obvious do I have to make it?"

His words shock me into silence. My vision has been so focused on Emily that I haven't even noticed Pete trying to get my attention. I never realised unobservant I am. I've learnt another new thing about myself. I try to recall any events that he might be talking about, but everything except Emily's face is blurry and in the background of my thoughts. "I didn't…I didn't know." My words are hollow and unnecessary. They aren't going to make Pete feel better at all. I thought me and Pete just 'got along' because we had to. I didn't think we really had anything in common, I never would have suspected that there was anything other than toleration, or maybe friendship at a push between us. To be perfectly honest, I thought he hated me.

"How are we going to repopulate the planet if

you won't even look at me?" I'm forced to gaze right at him, and it's immediately clear that this last comment was a dark joke. He has a weak smile on his lips but the tears are still dripping from his eyes. I want to hug him, but I don't know if that's the right thing to do. Will that give the wrong impression?

Soon, without speaking, Pete stands up and stalks off. I follow meekly behind, lost in the ocean of my own thoughts. I've been so thrown by his confession that I completely forgot to suggest returning to the base. We continue this way for a couple of hours, for miles until we reach the edge of the town.

We stop dead still. I'm trying to assess the danger, trying to figure out how many zombies are left here. Can they smell us? They certainly haven't immediately been drawn to our location, in any case. I wonder again if they are dying out. I'm sure Emily's theory is correct. It seems that we're in a lot less danger than I first thought.

"Shall we?" I ask gently, still wanting to return to our home as quickly as possible. Even if it *is* pretty safe, I don't fancy being out here in the dark.

Pete lets out a huge sigh and turns to face me. "I don't really know what we need, to be honest, Alyssa. I didn't really come out here for that." I nod; I'd already worked that much out. "I need to go home, back to where I live…well, lived before all of this happened. Losing Randy just reminded me of losing my family. They died by AM13 of course, but it still brought it all back." He huffs loudly, gearing himself up to say more. I start to panic, is he going to tell me that he's come here to commit suicide? Or stay at his home, is he really ditching the group? "Sorry that I've brought you all this way for this. I've spent all my time trying *not* to remember my family, and it's worked well, too well. Now I can't even picture what they look like. I thought I needed to forget about them to survive, but it isn't working anymore. I need something, anything. A photograph, a letter. I need a memento of my previous life. Do you know what I mean?"

I nod again, turning away so he doesn't see the sadness filling my expression. I've had the same problem. When I try to think of Lexi, I only see the zombie version of her. It's as if my little sister never existed in her human form. "Let's go," I whisper, not wanting to breakdown myself. I half wonder if I should go home too, while we're here. Maybe I should collect something too, but I know I'll be faced with Lexi's corpse and I don't know if I'll be able to walk out on her a second time. I can't risk that, it's unwise for so many reasons.

We move quickly and quietly, but it seems unnecessary. We don't encounter any zombies, but we do find a few corpses. These seem to be the dead bodies of the previously infected, but they're in such a state it's difficult to tell. They could've simply been eaten and left behind. Last time we were here; it was absolutely full of zombies. Did they all move on or are they all as dead as the few we've seen? Without a food source to keep them going, could their bodies really be failing them? I wish I knew for sure.

Finally we reach a small terraced house, and I

can tell by the way Pete's whole demeanour changes that this is the place. His shoulders tense up and his breaths become laboured. Sweat droplets start falling from his forehead. I wonder if there's something else in there, something else that he 'needs to do' that he hasn't told me about.

Before I can question him, he starts speaking in a cracked voice. "You wait here. I won't be long." He doesn't take his eyes off the building the whole time he's speaking. He doesn't look at me once.

I shrug my shoulders, having no need to argue. "Yeah, sure." As I watch him leave, I pray that this helps him get his act together. I know the group will never go back to the way it was without Randy, but we need to get some semblance of normality. We have to carry on, we've made it this far and we need to continue. We can't lose everything now. Not when we've worked so hard.

I have a feeling that he'll be inside for a while, so I scan the area for any potential threats, even though I know I won't see any. I can't shake my need to be vigilant. I sit on the fence at the edge of Pete's old garden and allow my mind to wander, imagining what the future holds for me and the rest of us. I envisage great things, especially for myself and Emily. I picture us surviving through the zombie apocalypse successfully, coming out of it better and more powerful. Then I start to wonder how our relationship will progress if it ever ends, if AM13 is finally cured. Will we be able to make it work in 'real life'? Will we get married; have children, live together forever? I just have no idea about life outside of this crazy little world anymore and that's petrifying.

Pete's footsteps from behind me drag me out of my imagination. "Hey, everything all right then?" I whip around, pleased that we can now leave, but to my surprise it's the rotting face of a familiar woman right in front of me, only a few inches away.

I know her, but at the same time I really don't.

"Mum…?" I pant, standing upright. "Mum, is that…is that you?"

Her skin is blackened, her veins dangling from her arms. Her mouth is filled with blood and broken, yellow teeth. Her eyes are bloodshot, her irises completely white. Her long dark hair, which was always very similar to mine, has practically vanished, leaving just a few dreadlocked strands behind.

As she snarls and moves, she leaves a trail of organs and chunks of flesh behind her. She moves slowly, so slowly it's almost as if it's happening in slow motion, but still I can't move. I'm so stunned that I'm frozen to the spot. Much as I want to run, I can't. She's so close, but if I acted quickly enough, I could probably get out of the way.

"Mum, I…?" My brain is acting irrationally, as if it wants to actually have some sort of conversation with this beastly version of my mother.

Come on, get moving! I think, but it gets me nowhere. My feet have become lead weights, firmly sticking to the ground below, my body solid stiff in a rigid position. I can't shout or even scream. I need to do something, *anything* to get myself away from this disgusting scent, before I vomit with the spores of decay sitting calmly in my throat.

She continues to move, and I remain stuck in one place.

This is the woman I resented for most of my life. Then when she left, I was angry, followed closely by incredibly hurt. Seeing her like this has brought all of these emotions to the surface once more. I see my hand reaching out towards her, but I can't feel it happening—as if my limb has completely disconnected from my body. It brushes against the gooey skin on her face as she moves closer, stripping her cheek of even more flesh. She doesn't flinch, or even seem to notice the pain that this should be causing. She just keeps coming for me.

Everything I know about zombies just abandons my mind as we stand there face-to-face. All I feel is a hollow sadness that *this* is what has become of the woman that gave birth to me.

It seems that she doesn't share in this sentimental moment with me, because before I can even blink an eye, her teeth have sunk deep into my cheek.

The pain snaps something in my brain and my legs finally start to push back. I continue to run until I'm hiding around the side of one of the buildings. I pant heavily, my heart pounding violently, blood pouring from my body, as I look around to see if she's followed me. To my relief, something else has taken her attention in the other direction. It's as if I never even existed to her. She's just ruined me, killed me, and then moved on to something else. My own mother.

I stagger back onto the street, agony radiating through my entire body. My vision starts to blur and the throbbing in my brain makes it difficult to get my head together, to plan my next move. I slump to the ground, desperate to cry. Am I going to become a zombie now? It's too much for me to contemplate. I can't believe this has happened to me. It's so unfair, everything I've survived and fought against, everything I've achieved during this awful time was all for nothing. I'm a fighter. I've worked myself to survive this world perfectly, so how the hell has *this* happened to me? I can't understand it. Not at all.

"Why, Mum?" I mutter, unable to contemplate that she just wouldn't know who I am, that she could just do that to me.

The next time I open my eyes, Pete's face is close to mine. So close that I manage to get a really good look at him. He's covered in blood, his face his full of purple grime. He's green, but pale at the same time almost as if he could vomit at any moment. Has he killed someone? Is that what he's been off doing? Maybe he saw what happened to me, and killed my mum. He's backing away from me, muttering under his breath. "No, no, no."

I try to speak, to plead with him to help me, to stay with me. I'm frightened. I'm more terrified than I've ever been before. I'm going to change; I'm going to become a zombie. I'm going to die. I need to accept these facts but they're unbearable. How do you tell yourself that you're actually going to cease to exist and there's not a single damn thing that you can do about it? It's insane; it feels as if it's happening to someone else, anyone else. Just not me. Is this what an out of body experience feels like? I feel like I'm floating on a wave of sheer torture. It's making me sick, but I can't get off. I'm struggling and fighting, but something is pinning me down, keeping me locked in one place.

Everything I was thinking about before this happened no longer matters. All of my wild plans, my silly worries, none of it will transpire. I have no future. My time, my life ends here. Right here in this moment. I'm too young for this. I had so much promise, so much potential. I was finally becoming someone worth something. I was becoming invaluable to the human race. Now look at me. I'm going to die before I can even live. I've fought and achieved and now I won't get to reap the benefits of everything I've done. I'm done for, I'm a goner. I'm dead. I want Pete's arms around me, I want him to hold me and tell me that everything's going to be okay.

Even though it isn't.

I allowed my own stupidity, my own emotions, to kill me, just like everyone I criticised before. I've received my comeuppance and it's a terrible thing. Everyone always used to say that karma was a bitch, and now I'm proof of that. I hate to be the evidence of such a cliché, and yet here I am.

Pete is gone, long gone. I can just about see him in the distance. I must be lying on the ground because everything looks wrong; it's all distorted, sideways. I can hear him shouting, but I can't understand the words. None of that matters anymore. Nothing. The pain, it's too intense. I didn't know it was possible for every single atom in your body to hurt like knives stabbing. I want to die. I want to die right now.

Oh Emily. I need you now more than ever.

Where are you, Emily?

CHAPTER 52

End

DR. JONES

Where am I? What's going on?

It's dark. It's really dark. I can barely see to write. Why am I even writing? Surely there isn't any point. I guess I just don't know what else to do. I've written for so long. I guess I always thought if I died, someone could read it, publish it, and let others know the hell I've had to suffer. Is that vain? To think anyone would be interested in what I have to write? I don't know. It's vain to think I had any worthy ideas I'm sure, but a small part of me still does. How can I still think I'm important after all of this?

What happened? I can't really remember anything. I think I got knocked out pretty quickly into the proceedings. I think, I don't know. Did the plan work? Did the three infected get into the boardroom? Why don't I know? Why can't I remember? I need to get my brain working. I need to recall the events. If it didn't work, then we're all fucked. If it did, why am I here? And where am I?

It's too black. It's dark. It's dark.

* * *

Where's Jason? I miss Jason. We've been together for so long that the empty space he's left behind is big. Too big. It's so dark here, and without him I'm actually frightened. I'm afraid. I don't know what to do with myself. He's like a missing limb.

Where am I? What's going on? Why can't I remember what happened? Everything hurts. Everything aches. Was I beaten? Am I infected? I don't know anything. Come on, brain, don't fail me now! I need you. I need to know what happened. I need to know if my revenge worked out.

Ashley. Where's Ashley? Did I do what I was supposed to? Did I kill her? I would remember if I had, wouldn't I? I'd remember ending my wife's life. If I didn't then I've left her to continue being abused. I'm a fucking loser that deserves nothing more than death. I didn't even do what I was supposed to. I let my wife down. And my daughter. I know for a fact that I never got to her. I never saved her from this nightmare, this hell hole.

Ashley. Dear God, Ashley, I'm so sorry. I've been a shitty husband right until the last moment. I didn't even put you out of your misery. I need them to be dead so they can't do anything else to you. Are they dead?

* * *

This room is damp and smelly. I've been trying to find something sharp—glass maybe?—to slice my wrists with. I've been down here for hours, maybe even days. I need it to stop. I want to end this. I need to end this on my own terms. I don't want to be controlled anymore. The board has stripped me of everything. Every single thing. My life is my own; I need to be the one to end it. I need to be the one who decides when I die. I can't stand the guilt, the constant worry. I want to take the easy way out.

I think it's safe to assume that the plan failed and I'm being held captive in here. The more I think about it and try to remember, that's the only logical conclusion I can come to. I'm scared. So unbearably frightened. What are they going to do to me? They won't just kill me. They could have done that already, no they're going to make me pay. They're going to do worse to me than they've ever done to anyone. I'm going to be a special case for torture.

I'm so fucking scared. So scared. The anticipation is worse than anything. This, right now, is more difficult than if they were right here in front of me, slicing my head off my neck.

I know what the monsters are capable of and I don't want it, any of it. I can't cope with the thought of it. The expectation, the waiting. I need to die. Knowing that death is your preferable option is awful. If I'm dead, they can still do things to my body, but my mind, my soul, my personality will be somewhere else entirely.

I need to die before they come down here and destroy me. How can I die?!

Please, if there is a God, please help me die. I need you, I've never needed you before, but now I do. Please help me end this, and escape from here.

* * *

I'm so hungry. My throat is dry. I don't

know how long I've been down here. I keep sleeping, or passing out, I'm not quite sure. I feel weird. Tired all the time. I could be losing myself to exhaustion, I don't know. I've never experienced this kind of deprivation before. I don't know anything anymore. Maybe they're just going to leave me to die. Leave me to starve like an abused animal. It's awful, it'll be agonising, but considering what they could do to me, I have to be glad I suppose. I wish it would be quicker, you know?

The pain is immense. I don't want to cope with it anymore. Is this what the victims of AM13 felt like? Am I experiencing what they went through? How ironic that I wanted them to feel it, and I'm suffering it instead. I'm about to become just another mindless victim of this fucking virus.

This needs to end, but I no longer have the energy to end it. My wrist hurts and instead of conserving my energy, I'm wasting it writing it all down. What does that tell you? I know too much. I just know...

It's all just...

* * *

Melody. Oh God, Melody, I'm so sorry. I let you down.

I let you down.

I let you down.

I love you; I love you and your mother so much. You're my world. I need you here. I wish you were here with me. Oh Melody, I'm so sorry for everything I did. This is my fault, you know that, don't you? Your mum didn't leave you, I made her disappear. If you have to blame anyone, make sure it's me. I'm sorry. I'm so very sorry. Why did any of this have to happen? You are too young for such loss, for such misery. You need to carry on and build a better life for yourself, I couldn't do it but you can.

I don't think I'll last much longer and I just wanted you to see what I do. I might die here, but it doesn't matter. I'm not fit for life, I'm too—

Anyway, I'm not good anymore. I'm bad. The world doesn't need badness anymore, there's too much of it. I'm bad. I'm one of the worst. I didn't start out that way; the badness sort of crept up on me. I didn't even see it happening. I didn't even know I was becoming evil until it was far too late. I don't know if it was the science that sent me to madness or if it was the board members. I don't want to blame anyone else anymore. I've accepted that I'm to blame for everything bad that's happened. I'm sorry, Melody, your old man isn't a hero, he's a villain. No child should have to accept that.

I feel like I can see things. Nice things. Pleasant things, it's such a lovely change from all that I've been through. Are they real? Maybe they're in my head. My head hurts. It's so full of...things. Am I crazy? If I am then it's better than being sane. This is the happiest I've felt in a long time. It's all finally coming together.

I think I can see you now. Is that you,

Melody? I'm over here.

I'm here.

I'm here.

* * *

Is it over yet? Am I done?

I think I'm dead...I could laugh manically with exhilaration. It's finally happened. I've finally died. I'm probably going to hell though. If heaven and hell even exists. I'm not destined for eternal happiness. How can I be after what I've done?

I'm bad, aren't I? I'm one of the worst guys there are. I deserve eternal damnation, don't I? Don't I?

Am I done? What's that I can see? Is it a light? A door opening? A person?

Has it happened yet?

CHAPTER 53

ALYSSA

The pain didn't last forever. In fact, I can barely remember the pain at all anymore. I almost wonder if I imagined it. Maybe I was just frightened, and what I thought I felt was a by-product of that.

The virus is consuming me quickly, really quickly. I'm slowly completely losing myself, becoming just another empty vessel. I assume it must have been the fact that my neck was bitten. I bet Emily would theorise that because it was close to my brain, it reacted with me quicker. Or something like that.

I never thought it would be me. I was *so* close to surviving the zombie apocalypse, it's so frustrating. I see dead zombies everywhere I go now, and it's quite depressing knowing that someday that'll be me. I remember being certain that I was fully equipped for the zombie apocalypse. I assumed that I'd be the best person, the one who'd survive it. How wrong can one person be? Although maybe being like this is preferable that what I will become. A bunch of dead mush on the floor for someone to scrape their shoe along.

Just look at me now. I'm revolting. I stink; my skin is so grey that it's almost black. Occasionally bits of me fall off. I turn around to witness the trail of flesh, grime, and organs that leave me. Everything is almost gone already. In the rare moments when I can still experience a glimpse of myself, this whole thing becomes too much to bear. I hate this, I despise everything about it. I desperately wish I could turn back time and go back to my life. The one I had before. Not before the apocalypse, but with Emily. That's when I was happy. That's when I was settled. It's such a shame that I'd only just discovered myself, just to lose myself all over again. How ironic to die just as I'd finally found a life.

When I first started to feel myself turning, I made myself get up and I walked with purpose until I found my mother—the woman that did this to me. I tore her to shreds, the way I should have done before she got her disgusting teeth into me, making me what I am now. Nothing, in fact I'm less than nothing. Nothing would be preferable to this. She was easy to destroy. Ripping her limbs from her body, leaving her a pathetic, shambolic mess. It was simple. Frustratingly easy, I could have done it when I was alive, she still would've proved no challenge for me. If only I hadn't allowed myself to get sentimental...what a fool!

After that, I had no idea what to do with the rage and the bloodlust that was slowly becoming my entire personality. I needed to redirect, to find something new to focus on. I needed a mission, in the same way I did before I was bitten. I needed a purpose; I guess that part of me will never leave.

And I've found it.

Occasionally I stand outside the RAF base, waiting for Pete to show his ugly mug. I'm going to kill him for what he did to me. I'm going to make him pay. It's his fault I got bitten, that I lost everything. I was only outside because of him, and he had the audacity, the indecency to leave me behind, to go through all that torture by myself. I think about all of this, getting myself so impatient and enraged waiting for him to appear.

I'll make him regret the day he ever met me, never mind the day he left me to die. What I did to Mum is *nothing* compared to what I'll do to him. I plan his death over and over, changing the details as I do. Some days I want to force him to watch me devour his intestines, to make him suffer painfully. Other days I want to merely bite him and detach his limbs as I watch him turn. Then he'll be like me, but with even less control. He'll be desperate to act in the way that I am, but without the ability to move. In that scenario, I watch him become just like me with glee. I make him see what he left me to endure.

But then time passes, and I forget myself for a while. I've 'woken up' in many places. Some I don't know, and others are very familiar to me; the church and the B and B. When I'm outside the building that I spent the time inside by myself, in complete and utter solitude, I wonder if any of the rest of it *really* happened. I have a vague memory of being bitten by one of the residents that I found here when I first arrived, dishevelled and saddened from the disappointing airport trip. I recall lying in one of the soft, plush beds, changing painfully. I remember ambling down the dusty path, losing myself, arriving in the town to join the zombie army.

I don't know if that's real, or my other memories are the truth. I've always had a very vivid, overactive imagination, so realistically I'll never know. I guess if I did die at the B and B, that would explain why I never found E. But it also leaves me with no enemy, no one to target my negative emotions towards, so I just refocus my hate and think of Pete's stupid face. The one I'm going to rip off his body when I finally get my hands on him.

Plus, it also means I invented everything that happened with Emily. Is that possible? Could I really have invented the whole thing? That seems one step too far. The entire relationship was so far removed from my usual self; surely I couldn't have made it up. The feel of her lips is still raw on my skin, it must've been real. It just had to be.

I'm hungry. So very hungry. I spend most of my time lusting after human meat. But there isn't any here. None at all. I can't smell a single person. There aren't even any animals left to feast upon. Unfortunately, due to the lack of humans, it seems the zombies were surviving off of them for a while. Maybe that's why they're dying out. Nothing left to sustain them. I know I certainly feel weaker by the second.

Or maybe it's simply the fact that we're all

falling to pieces. Our bodies disintegrating before our very eyes. I suppose our ailing bodies can truly only take so much. It's not like we could continue to survive with absolutely no skin or flesh left on our bones.

Now that I think about it, Lexi really did get off easy. What I did to her saved her this misery. Any guilt that I felt deep inside is gone. She got herself infected and I killed her to save her from this shitty life. If I was a weaker person, I'd have ran and left her to disintegrate into this. It isn't fair that there isn't anyone to put me out of my misery. Then again, if I'm struggling to go on with AM13 coursing through my veins, my little eight-year-old sister would have suffered more than is even worth thinking about. Maybe I needed to suffer this, so she could die. I don't know if that makes any sense, but it's the way I feel from time to time.

All I care about now is lasting long enough to avenge myself, to kill Pete. I hate him with such a passion and I refuse to end up a mush of skin and bones, trampled into the ground, just like the others, until he's gone. When he's gone, nothing else matters. I can go, happy with my achievements.

Well, maybe not *happy*. I'll never be happy again. I'll never be alive again, so how can I be happy?

And if I find out that Pete is simply a figment of my imagination, then I have no purpose left. I have no reason to live. I might as well just die the pathetic, lonely death that I know is coming to me anyway.

CHAPTER 54

ETHAN

I'm scrubbing my arm repeatedly, even though my skin is cracked and bleeding. I just *need* to get this virus off me. I can see it, I can feel it. It's there, I just know it, and I can't have it yet. Not now, not until I've found Leah. That was the *plan* and I'm not quite there yet. I only stop when my other arm can't take it anymore; the aching is too intense to carry on. My breathing is hurting my throat but my desperation to continue cleaning myself has taken over everything else.

My body falls to the hard, cobbled ground. I'm devastated, but unable to cry. I have no liquid left inside me, I'm extremely dehydrated. I can't remember the last time I drank or ate anything. My skin is stretched so tightly around my ribs that it's painful; my veins are all protruding, darkened and failing. I'm starving myself to death, I know I am. I'm just far too scared to let anything pass my lips. The OCD that was once a terrible problem in my life has finally overcome me entirely. That's all I am now, all the rest of my personality has long gone. It's disappeared along with my will to live.

I stay slumped against a wall for hours on end, my body too tired from all the fighting with myself to go on. My brain is screaming at myself to get up, that if I stay here then I'll never get what I want. The infected will find me sooner or later, and my life will end of some crappy street corner, not too far from where I wanted to be. But for the very first time, my feet don't respond to anything my mind is saying. My legs are too feeble, my body to frail. My eyes just want to sleep. I can't listen to my doomsday voice, however much I actually want to.

My eyes start closing. I'm begging them to stop, to keep open, but they won't. If I can't see the danger, I won't know that it's coming. But then, maybe the time has come to give up and accept defeat. I'm done with this battle. Realistically, I knew it was unlikely that I'd manage to get to Leah, I've been far too weak for far too long. And there's only so long I'll be able to keep any of the rest of *them* away from me, I can only hope that I've got no idea what is happening when I die. I don't want to feel pain. And if I *do* end up like one of those beasts, rather than simply dying, I hope someone braver than me puts me out of my misery, even though I don't deserve it. I definitely don't deserve it, but I can still wish all the same. I had two chances to put the people I love out of their misery, and I didn't do it. I know I deserve the comeuppance from this, but I pray that I don't get it all the same.

Finally I prise my eyes open, unsure if I'm still living. To my surprise I see someone walking towards me—an infected? No, I'm not sure it is. This must be some sort of hallucination. That makes a lot of sense; it was bound to end up like this eventually. I smile weakly at the man in front of me. He's in military uniform and I can hear crackling voices. My mouth wants to speak, to say something, anything, but it's too late, my brain has already made the decision to shut down, leaving me completely hopeless…

CHAPTER 55

TRANSCRIPT OF PRIVATE BROADCAST:

PM William Parle and Corporal Thomas Cleary

Transcribed by Carla Barnes 28th April 10:30 a.m.

WP: "Corporal Thomas Cleary, are you there? Over."

TC: "Yes, sir, I'm listening. Over."

WP: "Okay, what I'm going to explain to you now is confidential information. For your ears only, so I need you to confirm that you're currently alone. Over."

TC: "Confirmed. Over."

WP: "Okay. Things have failed on this end. We had some [*pause*] issues with the scientist that couldn't be resolved. We can't afford another blunder after the Lockdown. The people who have taken control of other continents are assuming that we've become weak, and that puts us in a bad position for the future, if you understand what I mean. Rumour has it that a scientist in Russia has a cure. Our Intel hasn't been able to confirm or deny this yet, but either way it doesn't look good for us."

TC: "What happened to the scientist, sir?"

WP: "He won't be bothering us anymore."

[*8 seconds of silence.*]

WP: "He had an idea that victims of the virus are weakening. We think this might be correct, so this is where you come in. Over."

TC: "Understood. Over."

WP: "We need you and your teams to conduct a final 'clean up' operation of the entire country, if you will. If the infected are dying out and easier to kill, it shouldn't provide too much of a challenge for you. Do you follow? Over."

TC: "Understood. Over."

WP: "I want to make this perfectly clear. Every single person currently left in the UK is to be assumed infected. No questions asked. Do you read me? Over."

TC: "Understood. Over."

WP: "I'm trusting you on this, Thomas. I'm putting a lot of faith in your hands. We cannot have another failure on our hands. This has to be successful if we have any hope of ever rebuilding the UK. Don't let me down, Thomas. Over."

TC: "What will happen then, sir?"

[*4 seconds of silence.*]

TC: "I just like to know what I'm fighting for, sir."

WP: "We are going to start organising the UK first, mainly because it's an island. Easier to keep anything 'unwanted' out. Then we will get everyone settled there as a temporary measure, whilst we get to work on the rest of Europe. This is going to be a lengthy operation, but it's the only way forward. We're hoping that the longer time goes on, the less work we'll have to do in each place."

TC: "Not to speak out of turn, sir, but why not stay where you are for the time being?"

WP: "For two reasons. One, it's no longer safe here. We've lost a lot of our board members in an unfortunate [*pause*] episode of late and a side effect of that is the camp is becoming unsettled. If I may be honest with you, Thomas, the issues are becoming too challenging to handle. The riots are becoming bloody and it's hard to regain control afterwards."

TC: "Sorry to hear that, sir."

WP: "This camp is too small for all of the people it's holding. These people need to be spread out and separated. The quicker, the better. I don't know how much longer we can continue here. Government secrets are being revealed with unpleasant consequences."

TC: "Are we still having a 'government' style system, after everything that's happened?"

[*9 seconds of silence.*]

TC: "Sorry, sir, I didn't mean that to sound disrespectful, I just thought [*pause*] with everything going on it was more [*pause*]. Sorry, sir, I shouldn't have spoken out of turn."

WP: "The second reason is we need to

show some sort of progress. For all the civilians, and to the other people in power. Europe needs to be seen as strong, as I've explained before. Over."

TC: "Okay, sir, so just to confirm your orders, anyone left in the UK is to be seen as a threat and killed. Then we must remove all of the bodies."

WP: "Burn all of the bodies. I need them disposed of in the most efficient way possible. I know it'll take time but you need to make absolutely sure that there is no one left. Another outbreak of this virus will finish us off. All of us. Over."

TC: "Understood. Your orders will be

followed out. My teams will be briefed efficiently and I will keep you updated with our progress. Thank you, sir. Over."

WP: "Good luck, Thomas. You're going to need it. You cannot fail. Over and out."

End of transcription.

ACKNOWLEDGMENTS

I would like to thank my friends and family, who have been a massive support to me whilst creating the AM13 Outbreak series. I'm also very grateful to everyone who read and enjoyed *Lockdown*. Your kind words have kept me going!

I would also like to thank Jennifer O'Neill, Lori Whitman and everyone at Limitless Publishing for all of your help, with special thanks to Toni Rakestraw, whose editing was invaluable.

ABOUT THE AUTHOR

Samie Sands is a 30 year old freelance graphic designer who has recently decided to follow her lifelong dream and use her creativity in a new way by writing.

She has a degree in Media Studies and PR and has already had articles published in a number of e-zines, including one of the most popular pieces at Zombie Guide Magazine. She has also had a number of her short stories included in some very successful anthologies.

She lives in a small seaside town in the UK, but loves to travel to gain inspiration from new places and different cultures. To follow Samie's work, please check out her website http://samiesands.com.

Facebook:
http://www.facebook.com/SamieSandsLockdown

Twitter:
http://www.twitter.com/SamieSands

Website:
http://samiesands.com/

Goodreads:
https://www.goodreads.com/SamieSands

66970209R00214

Made in the USA
Charleston, SC
05 February 2017